The Fisher Boy

The Fisher Boy

Darren Sapp

STEP PUBLISHERS
Accra, Ghana

THE FISHER BOY
Copyright © 2015, Darren Sapp

ISBN 978-9988211325

Published by
STEP PUBLISHERS
P. O. Box AN 11150, Accra-North, Ghana
stepwriters@gmail.com. www.stepbooks.org
Tel. +233 (0)302 513487

Cover design and page layout by
Sam Nyarko-Mensah (samadonia@yahoo.com)

In Memory of
Gp Capt. (Dr) Sam Annankra
. . . a man after God's own heart

There are many to thank for supporting me on this project. My wife Holly and children Kevin, Brandon, Jordan, Jadyn, and Megan for cheering me on and enduring my long trips to Ghana. Thanks to Sam & Esther Annankra, Francis & Cecilia Osei, and Rev. Moses Ocquaye-Nortey who have been incredible mentors. Thank you, Jeff Hughes and Nick Woodall for leading me to Ghana.

Thomas Woodall produced an incredible documentary, *Following the Fatherless*, that served as the catalyst for this book.

Tom Davis' *Priceless* and Harriet Beecher Stowe's *Uncle Tom's Cabin* have inspired me.

Dorcas Osei, Akua Tambo, and Bernard "Kofi" Ofosu-Appiah are incredible ministry partners and also served as beta readers.

The following answered my numerous questions: Donald Osei, Autumn Buzell, DK, Raphael, Amanda Tambo, Winnie Tambo, Lewis Fiadjoe, Joseph Mensa, and Grace Wobil Sedor.

Thanks to Mary Demuth, Leslie Wilson, Anne Mateer, and my critique group as well as the members of scribophile.com for your critiques. Thanks to Mary Norsworthy and Debbie Vines for proofreading.

I want to thank so many for shaping my thoughts through your service to orphans: Innocent Donu, Bernard Fianka, Romona Testa, Rusty & Linda Simpson, Georgina Happy Crentsil, Emelia Ojo, Anita Gillespie, John & Stacy Omorefe (www.cityofrefugeoutreach.com), John Nyavor, Humphrey Patterson, Cecilia Nketia, Kwaku Adu-Wusu, Comfort Asare, Ralph Adjaho, the Ghana Christian Alliance for Orphans (www.ghanaorphans.org) and Brian & Debbie McIntyre.

ONE

"Every Ghanaian matters!" Stephen Ghansah paused at the press conference podium before making his final statement. "As you consider your headline, I would prefer you type that. I know that it will likely say, 'MP Stephen Ghansah announces bid for President of Ghana' or something similar."

The room at the Ghana Royal Hotel in Accra erupted with raised hands and shouts of random questions. Lights flashed from photographers' cameras.

Ghansah raised one hand. "Please, I must go now. Thank you for your time. I am sure we will talk again soon. And remember. Every Ghanian matters."

Reporters continued their questions but Ghansah ignored them and exited the stage, offering the proverbial wave and smile of a politician. The room quieted and the reporters mingled.

"Honourable Ghansah, why have you been so silent about your childhood? Is it true you were once a slave?"

Ghansah stopped and turned, noticing a young lady staring right back. The other reporters looked at her as well. They stared, no doubt at her audacity for asking this after the press conference ended. Poor etiquette.

Ghansah walked up to her. "Miss Danku, correct?"

"Yes, sir. I am Ama Danku of the *Ghana World News*." She stood a full foot shorter than Ghansah.

"Please, may we speak over here?" Ghansah gently touched her elbow and motioned her away from the group. "Is your question more about the silence or the story itself?"

Danku cocked her head. "Well, sir, I suppose it is both. Do you have something to hide? I've asked your classmates from the university and they know nothing."

"No." Ghansah laughed. "I have nothing to hide."

"Then why the silence?"

Ghansah laughed again. "No one's ever really asked before."

Danku lifted her hand to her chin. "Really, sir? No one asked after you scored the winning goal in the World Cup? No one asked while you were running for MP? No one asked why your father has a different last name? A certain Mr Boateng?"

Ghansah nodded. "Yes, most know Paul Boateng is my father by adoption. But my MP election went fairly uncontested. I simply faced little opposition and the intense questioning that comes with it. I suppose those days are over."

"Please, Honourable Ghansah. May we meet soon for a formal interview regarding your background?"

"To be honest, my story is quite painful. I do not relish the thought of reliving those memories."

Danku leaned towards Ghansah. "But sir, the public must know your background."

"Yes, you are correct." Ghansah folded his arms. "I've read your work on the polarisation of the two political parties. It is good. You have grasped the essence of my party's stance. One condition though—you must report my story as I tell it. No fabrication. No embellishment. For that, you have exclusive rights. Agreed?"

"Agreed." Danku smiled and nodded.

"Can you meet me tomorrow? My home, two o'clock, Miss Danku?"

"Yes, sir. That will be fine."

"William," Ghansah said, motioning to a staffer. "William. This is Miss Danku. She will meet me at my home tomorrow at two for an interview. Please provide her directions."

"Yes, sir," said William.

Ghansah extended his hand to Danku. "At your age—as I assume you are in your twenties—this presents quite an opportunity. I will expect your best work."

"Yes, sir. Of course," Danku said as she returned the handshake.

* * *

Ghansah—making preparations in the kitchen—heard his wife Grace greet their visitor at the front door of their East Legon home. "Miss Danku. I am Grace, Kwaku's wife. You are welcome."

Ghansah joined them in the den, holding a tray of cups and a teapot. "Miss Danku. You are most welcome. Would you like some tea?"

3

"Yes, thank you."

"I must admit, Honourable Ghansah, I expected a large home. A golden gate with ornate features. Barbed wire. Several security guards and a team of servants. This doesn't seem like the home of the would-be president."

Ghansah laughed, held up his hands, and motioned towards the walls. "Well, Miss Danku, we prefer simplicity."

"And your guard. He is elderly. Surely you need more security?"

"You mean Samuel? He is not much for security in a physical confrontation, but I assure you he is wiser than most. He does the job just fine." Ghansah sipped his tea. "Miss Danku, I am sure you have many questions and a certain direction you may want to take this interview. Am I correct?"

"Yes, of course, sir. Where were you born? What happened to your parents? How did you meet your adoptive father, Mr Boateng? All of these questions and many more."

"Miss Danku, allow me to start at the beginning. My story could have been a tragedy. It's difficult to hear. You may be angered at times. But allow me to tell it and you will understand the difference that Ghanaians can make in one another's life. How God works in the lives of people. And why I chose "Every Ghanaian Matters" as my campaign slogan. Ghansah smiled. "Agreed?"

Danku smiled back. "Agreed."

TWO

My father said, "Always look for God" whenever we faced adversity, triumph, despair, or any difficult situation. He said it for the last time only a few hours before he died. That was 23 years ago. That is when my most difficult days began.

"I'm off for work," he said, hugging my sister and patting me on the head. He worked road construction in Kumasi.

As he opened the door, Mummy just looked out the window. She suffered from depression due to our economic hardship and lack of family support. We had no living grandparents. My father's brother worked somewhere in the North but we had not heard from him in years.

Father, sensing our sadness, said, "Always look for God." Wearing an orange safety vest and carrying a hard hat, he walked to the end of the street to catch the *trotro*.

"Mercy. Kwaku. Eat your porridge," Mummy said. My parents named my older sister Mercy in honour of God's mercy towards us.

Our typical day entailed walking through the neighbourhood selling tea bread that Mummy had made before I headed off for school. For a girl of 14, and me, a boy of 11, we made a good team, but tea bread only earned us so much. Mercy desperately wanted to attend school again, but our parents only had funds for one of us. She had recently quit school to look for work.

The knock on the door that late afternoon startled us. No one ever knocked on our door. Mummy opened it to find a policeman standing there with his hat under his arm.

"Yes, sir?" Mummy said.

"Are you the wife of Elijah Ghansah?"

"Yes, sir."

The policeman dipped his head. "I regret to inform you that your husband has been killed. An articulated truck ran him over, killing him instantly. All I have to give you is his wallet. I'm sorry."

My mummy received the wallet and closed the door as the policeman turned and briskly walked away.

Mercy cried, "Nooooooo!"

Mummy walked over and stared out the same window as when Father left. I ran over and hugged her as my tears flowed. She returned no hug. Mummy was not a cold person. Her shock left her numb. Unfeeling. Detached. No tears fell from her cheek.

Our loud cries calmed and there occurred a long silence. "There is nothing left for us in Kumasi. We shall make our way to Accra to find work," Mummy said.

I laid in bed that evening next to Mercy. She held me tight. I only thought one thing. Where was God now?

* * *

No visitors came the day after Father died. No one would post bills around town announcing a "Call to Glory." No family came for a funeral. Mummy finally opened the wallet to find a few cedis and some photographs of us. She went to see Father's employer who gave her some money for Father's work and paid our bus fare to Accra.

"I will miss home," I said.

"Why? It is the fourth home we have had in two years," Mercy said, as she packed the last of our belongings. We could carry all we owned.

"I mean Kumasi, the place of my birth." I began to cry, thinking of Father.

Mercy rubbed my arms. "Do not cry, Kwaku. We have to start a new life in Accra." She inherited her resilience from Father.

The bus ride to Accra normally takes five hours. A flat tire and overheated engine doubled the time. I filled the time observing the small towns and villages. I wondered how children in the mud huts lived. Their life may have been simple. But I assumed they shared that simple life with a father. My sadness remained but my eyes widened as we entered the city of Accra. So many new things to see. Tall buildings. The ocean. So many new people to meet. Accra seemed busy like Kumasi but the capital seemed to carry an importance.

"Where will we sleep, Mummy?" I asked.

Mummy held her stare out the window and coughed. "A hostel or guest house of some sort. Then we must find work. Don't worry, Kwaku. You will be back in school soon."

Her depression deepened, but she still held my hand. She still tried to offer an occasional uplifting moment.

We did find a hostel on arrival in Accra, but the cramped conditions made me long for a place of our own. Our room had two small beds. Mercy and I shared one while Mummy slept in the other. We took turns with other hostel residents using the washroom—one per hallway. I fetched water each morning and Mercy made our porridge. After a few days, Mummy found part-time cleaning work for her and Mercy at a local hotel, while I stayed at the hostel. I wanted to provide as well.

I approached the hostel owner. "Sir, do you have any work for me? I am strong. I can fix things. I can clean."

He looked down at me over his reading glasses. "Sorry, young man. I have grown men employed and hardly enough work for them." He turned to walk away. "You should be in school."

"We cannot afford the school fees. Please, sir, I can work as hard as a grown man. Look." I reached down and lifted a box full of junk in a desperate show of strength.

He sighed. "Would you like to read some books?"

My eyes widened and I smiled. "Yes, sir! I love to read."

Walking to the office, he said, "They are my son's old books. You may borrow them, but you must take care of them and bring them back." He grabbed one from the shelf. "Have you read *Charlotte's Web*?

"What, Sir?

"*Charlotte's Web*. It's an American children's book. Please, go to your room and read," he said, handing me the book and shooing me away.

"Thank you, sir. I will take care of it."

I thought the cover odd. A little white girl with animals and a spider. Animals did not seem of particular interest to me, but I decided I could try it.

I loved reading in school and Mummy made sure I continued until she raised funds for my school fees.

Those first few days in Accra soon turned into weeks. I fought boredom by reading, walking around, and playing with a few other children living in and near the hostel. Mummy and Mercy came home each day exhausted. I desired interaction with them, but they only wanted rest.

"Mummy, when will we move to a place of our own?" I asked.

She rubbed her head and coughed. "I do not know, Kwaku. I hardly earn enough money for us to eat and pay for this hostel." Her cough had worsened over the last week and she complained of fever.

"But Mummy, what about the money I earn?" Mercy asked.

"Child, they only pay us half for you because of your age."

Mercy placed her hands on her hips. "That is not fair. I work as hard as anyone."

Mummy smiled. "Yes, you do. You are a hard worker. You—" Her cough interrupted her sentence.

I grabbed Mummy's hand. "We must take you to a doctor," I said.

"No. We cannot afford—" Mummy fainted and fell to the floor. We lifted her onto the bed.

"Kwaku, get the hostel owner," Mercy said. She slapped at Mummy's hand in an effort to revive her.

I ran down the hall as fast as I could. The hostel owner's wife noticed my pace. "Child, stop running."

"Ma'am, my Mummy has passed out."

The hostel owner's wife knew a nurse that lived nearby and asked her to come to see Mummy. She had no doctor bag. No instruments. As Mum began to wake and mumble, the nurse felt her head.

"I am afraid your Mum's fever is very high. I have seen this many times. She has typhoid."

Mercy stepped forward. "Please, ma'am. Give her some medicine."

"It is too late for that, child. Try to keep her head cool and give her water."

Mercy pleaded. "What about a clinic or hospital?"

The nurse shook her head. "No. It's too late."

For the next week, Mercy and I took turns tending to Mum. She spoke nonsense sometimes but at other moments, spoke with clarity. She had rarely spoke of Father since his passing.

Mercy tried anything to raise Mummy's spirits. She lightly stroked Mummy's hair. "Mummy, tell me about Father." She rubbed her arm. "Tell us a story about Father."

I lay on the bed next to Mummy and held her hand tightly. I did not really know how to pray, but I did so earnestly. We had not been to church since arriving in Accra. We had no pastor to help us pray. I pleaded with God to hear my prayers and heal my mum.

Mummy struggled to speak. "Always look for God."

I sat up and looked at Mercy. "That is what Father always said. Maybe this is the hope we prayed for."

THREE

Mummy lasted three more days. We never had the opportunity to say goodbye to Father. His death shocked us, but Mummy's death seemed worse. We watched the life slowly sucked from her body. And then we had no parents.

Mercy clutched her hands and rocked back and forth. "No, Mummy. Please, Mummy."

I whimpered at the foot of the bed. "This cannot be happening."

The hostel owner heard our cries and entered our room. "What is this noise? Is she gone?"

"Yes, sir." Mercy said through tears still holding Mummy's hand.

"This body must be removed. I will call for someone." He started to walk out the door and said, "Your Mum was one week behind on the rent. Do you have it?"

I never learned the hostel owner's name. He seemed kind to us before but then so cold. In spite of our grief and desperate situation, he had no empathy for us.

Mercy reached for Mum's bag. "We have only a few cedis."

"Give me what you have." He counted the money. "You will need more to stay longer. If not, you will have to be out by morning. I'm not operating an orphanage. I will be closed if renters do not pay."

Mercy stood up. "Sir, where will we go?"

"Go stay with family. An uncle or aunt."

"But sir, we do not have any."

He threw his hands up. "This is not my problem. You must leave in the morning."

I began to cry. Mercy held me. "Don't worry, Kwaku. I will find us some place." My sister's bravery reminded me of Father.

As I had when Father died, I went to sleep that night in Mercy's arms. Surely we would find God soon.

* * *

The next morning, the hostel owner's wife burst in our room. "You need to gather your things and leave. Paying renters will be here soon." She began packing mother's things. "I will take these as payment."

Mercy resisted, but the woman pushed her away.

"You have ten minutes to leave or I will call the police."

Mercy tried to act brave but seeing Mummy's things taken away must have been too much. She dropped to her knees and cried inconsolably.

"Mercy, we can find something. We can find someone to help us." I rubbed her back. "We shall look for God. That is what Father told us to do. Even Mummy said it sometimes."

"No, Kwaku. There is no God. No God would take Father and Mummy from us in less than one month. No God would make us helpless orphans."

The hostel owner's wife returned. "Go. You must go now," she said, pushing us out the door. "Make your way to Agbogbloshie. You can find work as a *kaya* or something else."

"Come, Kwaku," Mercy said, grabbing my hand. We walked out onto the street and Mercy said, "This way."

"Where are we going?"

"To the hotel where Mummy and I work. They will help us."

I had never seen the hotel. It took us an hour of walking through markets and busy streets to arrive. I suddenly realised that Mum and Mercy made this trip six days per week and sometimes seven. We approached a huge gold-coloured gate. Curved spikes topped the walls. A sign on the building said Yendi Hotel. I could see a huge white building hidden behind some trees.

The security guard stopped us. "Where are you going, miss?"

"To work," Mercy said with confidence.

"Who is this boy?"

"He will work, too. We are going to see the manager."

The guard laughed at the thought. "You can try, but I doubt he will hire a boy." He opened the gate and allowed us to enter.

We walked in—Mercy carrying our one suitcase and me carrying a plastic bag with a few other items the hostel owner's wife had not stolen from us. The hotel grounds seemed alive with activity. Men walked about with briefcases as workers loaded their luggage in taxis. We walked past two white men talking to one another in the parking lot. I could not understand their English as they spoke too quickly. One of them looked at me with no emotion and the other smiled and nodded. We walked by the restaurant and the smell of food consumed me. I had not eaten since we ate the last of our porridge the previous day for breakfast. I stopped at the door and saw many people laughing and eating. It seems strange to think that only one day after losing Mummy, my main desire was food. I suppose my survival instincts took over.

"We must find the manager, Mr Lartey," Mercy said. She led us around the hotel with intensity. She seemed very much in-charge.

"Can we go eat in that restaurant?" I asked.

"Of course not. We have no money." She pointed. "There he is. Stand straight and act your best." The manager looked to be in a hurry walking down the hallway. "Mr Lartey."

"Yes." Mr Lartey wore a dark suit with striped tie. He wiped the sweat from his brow with a handkerchief. "What do you want?"

"Sir, do you remember me? I am Mercy. My Mum and I have been working here the last few weeks."

He folded his arms. "You mean that you did work here. What do you think happens when you do not show up for work? We have not seen you in a week."

"But, sir. My Mum became sick with typhoid and passed away last night. Please, may we stay here? I will work."

"Huh, you could not earn enough in one month to pay for a room here for one night. Besides, I only let you work here because your Mum begged me. Now go. You must leave."

"But, sir. Please. There must be some work for us. This is my brother, Kwaku. He is a hard worker. He is strong."

"I cannot have children working here. We are a respectable hotel." Then he smiled at Mercy. A strange smile. He looked at Mercy from head to toe and patted his brow again. "Maybe there is something."

Mercy perked up. "Yes, sir?"

"I will let your brother sleep in the storage building in the back. And you shall sleep in my room."

Mercy's mouth opened wide. She grabbed my arm and walked quickly away from Mr Lartey. "Come, Kwaku."

I resisted her. "Why are we leaving? Mr Lartey said we could stay."

"Because he is a bad man, Kwaku."

"I do not understand. He said—"

"You must trust me, Kwaku."

We exited the gate leading to the dirt road in front of the hotel. Mercy looked left and right. "This way."

I doubt she had any idea which way we should go but went on instinct. We walked for miles through the busy streets, wandering from one place to another. I noticed the occasional look from a passerby. Did they wonder who we were? Did they care? Were we mere street children to them? Everyone seemed so busy. They had purpose. They had a place to go. We had no place to go.

I pulled Mercy's hand. "Maybe we should ask some person where this Abeebushie place is. The place the hostel owner's wife said we should go."

"No, Kwaku. I will find us some place. She only told us that to get rid of us."

"But I am hungry. What will we eat?" I said rubbing my tummy.

The sun began to set and we had found no place to go. No prospects. People bustled about on their way home. Stores began to close.

Mercy yanked my hand and ran. "Come, Kwaku."

We approached a woman closing her shop. "Please, ma'am. We have no place to go. We have not eaten today," Mercy said.

"What do you want me to do, child? Where are your parents?"

"They are dead."

The woman looked at both of us for a long time and then patted my head. "Please, I have many children of my own to care for. But you may sleep in the doorway under the roof."

Mercy nodded. "Thank you, ma'am." We sat down in the doorway thankful that we had a roof over us as rain began to fall. Thankful we did not have to sleep on the dirt. Thankful for a glimpse of compassion.

A few minutes later, the woman returned. "Here are some biscuits and water."

"Thank you," we both said in unison.

"I do have to run my business and will need you to leave by morning. Understand?"

Mercy nodded. "Yes, ma'am. Where is this Agbogbloshie? We understand we may find work there."

The woman nodded. "Yes, you will find work. But be careful. There are many that would deceive you." She gently grabbed Mercy's chin. "Do you understand, child?"

Mercy nodded. "Yes, ma'am."

She proceeded to give us the directions and then left. I walked around the shop eating my biscuit. A dog trotting by stopped and looked at me. I noticed his rib bones protruding from his sides. He looked hungry, but I refused to give him my only food.

I noticed the sign on the shop. "Mercy, look at this funny name. Jehovah-Jireh. I do not understand."

Mercy stood next to me and looked. "Jehovah-Jireh Beauty Salon."

I cocked my head. "What kind of name is that?"

"I am not sure, Kwaku. Maybe something religious."

As I sat back down under the roof, I thought of one thing. We may not have found God. But he did provide us food and shelter that first night.

* * *

Mercy had made us save one biscuit and a little water to share for breakfast. We picked up our belongings and walked for several hours that morning before noticing a wide sewer.

"It smells here," I said. "We should keep walking."

Mercy approached a woman. "Ma'am, what is this place?"

"Agbogbloshie," she said and kept walking.

The area burst with activity. People and cars manoeuvring about and many balancing head trays while selling various goods. Boys pushed carts piled high with everything from engine parts to chickens. I noticed one main difference from other parts of Accra. Trash everywhere. That is when I knew why it smelled. As we walked farther, I noticed another difference. Many of the homes were mere shanties. One side might be sheet metal and the other side wood. Why would the hostel owner tell us to come here? This did not seem like a place where we would find prosperity.

A car honked and the driver yelled something at us. We could not tell where the street began and where it ended.

A girl that looked to be Mercy's age approached us. "You need a place to stay?"

Mercy nodded. "Yes. Can you help us?"

"Come with me." We followed her through rows and rows of shops and shanties for several minutes. The girl pointed to a shelf behind a shanty. "Leave your things here. I will show you where you can find food and work."

I began to set my bag down. Mercy extended her arm to hold me back. "Wait, Kwaku."

The girl insisted. "It's fine. No one will touch it. This is my place. We will be right back. You don't want to carry your things around to find work, do you?"

Mercy relented and we set our things on the shelf. The girl led us back through the maze of tiny structures. She began moving faster so that we almost had to run. Then, she turned a corner and disappeared. We never even learned her name.

Mercy put her hands to the side of head. "Oh, no! Our things. Our clothes. Father's wallet."

We ran back to the shanty and found our suitcase and bag gone.

"She tricked us," Mercy said.

It all happened so fast. I immediately thought of the warning from the woman who gave us the biscuits.

We stood there as people bustled around us. Smoke rose in the distance from burning debris. My nose reminded me of the stench. We proceeded to walk all over the shanty town that day, but never found the girl or our belongings. No money. No food. Nothing but the clothes on our backs. Less than 48 hours after Mummy passed away and we were truly alone. The sense of hopelessness overwhelmed me.

As the sun went down, we found no kind shop owner to provide us food and shelter. We sat down next to a pile of trash and Mercy held my hand. My stomach growled. My strong sister offered no encouraging words that night as we fell asleep using rubble for our pillow.

FOUR

I woke up the next morning to that now familiar stench but did not see Mercy. Has she been taken from me too? I panicked "Mercy! Mercy! Where are you?" I ran around the pile of trash. "Mercy!"

A hand grabbed me from behind. "Kwaku, I am here."

"Where did you go?"

"I went to find us work."

She handed me a plantain chip. I recoiled at its appearance. "Where did you find it? It has black spots and is soggy."

Mercy rolled her eyes. "Just eat it."

It tasted old and terrible, but I ate it. Although small, it satisfied my belly for the moment. But only a moment.

Agbogbloshie bustled with activity as people went about their morning business. A woman near me swept trash on the dirt, from one pile to another. I thought this seemed fruitless. Women walked by with head trays and some of them even had babies wrapped up on their backs. One boy rode by on his bike wearing a school uniform. He seemed so out of place in the mess. A young girl poured water into a small body of water that lay stagnant. The trash floated on top of it with no sense of purpose. The awful smell invaded my nostrils once again.

Mercy led me away from our home of trash for the night. "I found a lady that said you could work as a *kaya*. You will move goods on carts. She will let us sleep in her shanty and we can earn enough for food."

"What about you?"

"She said, 'Oh, you are so pretty. Heh, heh. I know how you can make good money,'" Mercy said in a mocking tone.

"What kind of work?"

"You would not understand, Kwaku."

We arrived at the place of work. Another shanty with a dirt floor. Several children stood around talking among themselves. A woman walked out eating tea bread and drinking cocoa. I licked my lips.

"Ma'am. Please, this is my brother, Kwaku," Mercy said, gesturing towards me.

The woman grabbed my shoulders. "Oh, you a strong boy, heh, heh. You will make a good *kaya*. You call me Auntie Agnes, understand?" She began and ended many of her sentences with a couple of short laughs.

"Yes, ma'am."

Auntie Agnes did not appear wanting for food. Her stomach stuck out and poked me as she touched my shoulders. She had her own bad smell. As bad as the smell of Agbogbloshie.

"Prince, come here," she said. A boy of my age ran over. "Prince, this is Kwaku. You show him the work." Prince nodded.

"Heh, heh. Mercy. You come with me and I will show you your work." Mercy frowned and looked off to the side.

We lost our parents. Our situation seemed hopeless. But this new day promised something different. Work. Shelter. Food. I had no idea why Mercy seemed discouraged.

"Come," Prince said. He walked quickly like everyone else in Agbogbloshie.

They all seemed in such a hurry.

"Listen, Kwaku. You do everything I say. I will show you how to work hard and we will get paid."

I liked Prince immediately. He talked and walked with confidence. He seemed to take his work seriously, but managed to smile as he talked with me.

We walked about ten minutes when Prince stopped us and knelt down. "See that man?"

"Yes."

"He is a bad man. Stay away from him."

I stood up and loudly said, "Why is he bad?"

Prince grabbed my shirt and pulled me down. "Shh. He will hear you. We will go this way." We walked around a few shops and continued back on the street. "He is a bully. He grabs boys and beats them for no reason."

"Why?"

"I don't know, Kwaku. He is bad or crazy or something. Maybe he takes their money. You listen to me. We must be smart and avoid certain people. I will show you. There are many that will steal from us or try to trick us. I know my way around." Prince pointed. "There is the place." We met a man surrounded by baskets of food.

"You are late, Prince."

"I am sorry, sir. I had to wait on this new boy."

"We'll get this loaded and deliver it. You will have to move fast." As we loaded the cart, I could only think of eating. As if reading my thoughts, the man said, "Hey, new boy. Don't think about eating this food. If you do, I will punish you."

"Yes, sir."

The empty cart already seemed twice as long and wide as me, but with the goods, it now seemed twice as tall as me.

"You push and I will steer," Prince said.

I pushed with all my strength and the cart finally moved. Unfortunately, we had to keep stopping because of all the people and cars in the way. It took us an hour to reach our destination and unload the cart.

"Phew . . . Are we through with our work?"

Prince laughed. "No, of course not. We have many more loads. We must go."

"How long have you worked as a *kaya*?" I asked, as we pushed the empty cart.

Prince looked up in the air. "Let me think. About one month."

"Do you live with Auntie Agnes?"

"No. I live with my grandmother in a shanty. We will go by there later. I will show you."

"Where are your parents?"

Prince, normally quick to respond, paused before answering. "I don't know my father. I never met him. My mother works at Osu carrying a head tray. Sometimes she lives with us, sometimes not."

"Why Osu? Why not here?"

"She makes more money at Osu. I don't know who she lives with."

We stopped again for traffic. "Why do you ask so many questions, Kwaku?"

"I am curious."

Prince laughed. "Some may think you are nosy."

We delivered our next load to a location much farther. The hard work and Prince's friendship distracted me from my sadness. I had hoped that Mercy's work gave her a similar distraction. Prince found us a place with running water to drink.

"Do you go to school, Prince?"

"Do you think I would work if I could go to school? My grandmother sent me to work so we could eat. She is almost blind and cannot work." Prince grunted as he pushed.

Due to our full cart, I could not see him.

"I want to go to school. I am 11 years old and have never been. I want to wear a uniform and learn to read," Prince said.

The cart abruptly stopped, and I smashed my face into it.

"Why did you stop?"

"Look." Prince pointed at two soldiers walking down the street.

They stood tall and proud. Their crisp uniforms had perfect creases with the pants tucked into their shining boots. They looked down at us and kept walking. We both stood up straight to mimic them.

"I want the school uniform. Then I want that uniform," Prince said.

We moved our loads all day in the hot sun and finished the last one as evening haze settled over the large open dump area. I saw no beauty in this dusk.

Prince led me back to Auntie Agnes' shanty. "I will see you in the morning, Kwaku."

Auntie looked at me with hands on hips. "Hey, boy, did you work hard today? Heh, heh."

"Yes, ma'am." Usually perky, my exhaustion caused me to respond quietly with my head hung low.

"Go eat some Banku and get some water. You earned your meal and mat today."

Mat? I hoped for a bed but she pointed to a mat on the dirt floor. I gave no argument and proceeded to eat my meal.

"Auntie Agnes. Where is Mercy?"

She cocked her head. "Who, boy?"

"My sister."

"Oh. Heh, heh. She is working. She will work into the night. You forget about her and go to sleep. You will start work very early."

I could not forget about Mercy. I certainly thought of my Father and Mummy. I thought of Kumasi. But as I lay on my mat, I worried about Mercy. What work would cause her to come back late into the night. Weakened in mind and body, I began to drift off to sleep.

I woke sometime later when Mercy walked in. She laid down slowly with her arms crossed, and I could tell she had been crying.

I sat up. "Mercy, what is wrong with you? What is this work?"

Mercy pushed me back down. "It is bad work, Kwaku. You are too young to understand. Go back to sleep."

* * *

"Get up, Kwaku." I woke to someone kicking my feet. "Get up. It is time for work." As my eyes opened, Prince came into view.

"It is dark outside," I said, rubbing my eyes.

"This is when we start work. Not every day. But today we have many loads." Prince began walking out. "Ask Auntie for some tea bread and come. We must hurry."

I looked next to me and there slept Mercy. She seemed peaceful. I had hoped she could rest today and not do the bad work.

"Prince, do you know the bad work they make my sister do? She must work late into the night and she only tells me it is bad work and that I will not understand."

"I don't know, Kwaku. You ask too many questions."

* * *

We pushed our cart and delivered our load much as the day before. I ate my meal of Banku and lay on my mat just as the evening before, then fell asleep without Mercy. I woke to a commotion.

"Get up, girl. Get up." Auntie Agnes kicked at Mercy who must have come in after I fell asleep.

"No." Mercy resisted. "No, I do not want to do that work anymore."

Auntie kicked her again. "You will work or your brother will be thrown out into the street." Auntie shook her finger. "I have a man that wants you, and you will give him what he wants."

"No," Mercy said. Auntie grabbed her hair and dragged her out of the room as Mercy continued her protests. "No! Ow! No!"

* * *

I told Prince the next morning what happened, but he had no answers. What could two young boys do? We continued pushing our cart.

After our first load, someone yelled. "Hey, boys."

Prince pointed to himself. "Me?"

"Yes. You boys. Come over," the man said. He sat in a large black car with the door open. He looked at another man sitting next to him and smiled.

"Prince, is that the bully who beats boys for no reason?"

"No. I don't know this man. Come." Prince motioned for me to follow.

"Hey, you boys work hard moving those loads?" He nodded and smiled at us while slightly focused on the chicken he devoured. His friend had money in stacks on his lap. He appeared to be sorting and counting it.

Prince stood up straight. "Yes, sir. We are very hard workers."

I stood up straight to match Prince.

"My name is Simon. I am looking for two hard workers for a special job for a few days. I will pay good money.

The workers I hire sleep in their own bed and eat in restaurants."

I began nodding.

"But maybe not you boys. I do not think you are strong enough."

Prince objected. "Sir, we are strong. We push the carts all day. We will work hard."

I nodded. "Yes. We will."

"But surely you make more money as a *kaya*. You want to keep that job, right?"

"No," Prince said. "We want to work for you."

"Very well. But we must drive there." He motioned for us to get in and threw his chicken bone on the ground.

Prince paused. "But, the cart. We must tell Auntie Agnes."

"Who? Oh, you mean the person you work for. Leave the cart. I will have someone take care of it and tell them you are working for me now."

Simon handed us some water. "Do you like chocolate?"

"Yes, sir," we said in unison. We looked at each other and smiled at our great fortune. In that moment, I forgot about my parents. About Mercy. About everything. My excitement consumed me. It did not occur to me to ask if Mercy could work with us. When we would return? What kind of work we would do?

Prince and I looked around as we drove through the city and after some time, out of the city.

"Mr Simon, where are we going?"

"The work is far. It will take us some time to get there."

"Just eat your chocolate and rest," said Simon's friend in the passenger seat.

After several hours, we came upon a large body of water settled among hills. I had never seen anything like it. I tapped Mr Simon on the shoulder. "What is this place?"

"Lake Volta. This is where you will work. It is beautiful. You will love it." Simon again smiled at his companion.

We stopped in a small village near a shanty similar to those in Agbogbloshie.

Simon turned off the engine and both men exited the car. "You boys stay in the car until I call for you."

We looked around and could see people in boats working with nets.

"You boys, come," Simon said, waving us over. "Stand up straight." He patted my shoulders. "See, I told you these boys are strong."

Another man in ragged clothes looked us over. Although tall and thin, solid muscles showed through his clothing. He folded his arms. "OK," he said, and reached in his pocket and gave Simon some money.

"You boys work for this man, here. You understand?"

Neither of us nodded. I certainly did not understand what was happening.

"Do you understand!" That time, Simon shouted. The kind man who gave us water and chocolate did not seem so nice now.

"Yes, sir," we both said feebly. My teeth began to chatter.

Simon chuckled with his friend and counted the money in his hands. They got in their car and drove off.

"You boys work for me now. You call me Master Ben."

FIVE

Master Ben spared no time putting us to work.

"John, come here," Ben said, and waved at three boys that lay under a huge mango tree.

One popped up and ran over as the other two looked on.

"Yes, Master Ben."

"John, this is—" Master Ben looked confused and turned to us. "What are your names, boys?"

"I am Prince."

I remained silent, still confused about what had happened, where I was, and why I was here.

Master Ben slapped my shoulder. "Speak up, boy. What is your name?"

"Uh…uh…I am Kwaku."

"This is John. Kwaku, you do the work he says. If you do not work, you will be punished. Now go." He grabbed Prince's arm, walked towards the other boys, and yelled at them, "Your rest is over. Get to work."

I followed John to the lake. He wore only short pants with no shirt and had muscles everywhere. His neck and shoulders seemed out of proportion to the rest of his body. I went in one boat with John while Prince fished in a different boat with the other boys. Prince's boat had writing on the side, but it had worn away so much I could not read it. My boat read Psalm 28.

A Bible verse? I thought.

A fishing net filled our boat with barely enough room for us to sit.

The lake smell filled my nostrils. Not a bad smell like Agbogbloshie, but not a pleasant smell either. The water looked somewhere between green and brown. Occasionally, a slight breeze blew across my face. Since everything happened so fast, it did not occur to me at the time that I had experienced my first boat ride. Hardly an enjoyable experience.

We paddled and paddled until we reached far onto the lake.

"We will put the net out here," John said.

I followed along as best as I could and had so many questions.

"How long—"

"Just do the work. You can ask questions later," John said.

It took us a long time to untwist and lay the net out in the water. We then paddled to a floating marker to pull in a similar net full of fish. My arms ached and my hands felt as if the skin would tear off. I pulled several times and sat down.

John looked at me. "Why are you sitting?"

"I am tired and need to rest."

"You cannot rest. Master Ben might see you sitting. He will punish you and punish me. Get up and pull. Get up."

I obeyed as much as possible but sat a few more times. The net came in with several fish. The boat filled with water so we bailed out as much as we could and then paddled back to shore.

We pulled our fish from the net and put them in a bucket. Women near a shanty called for us to bring them the catch for processing. The other boys had already returned.

Master Ben walked quickly towards us in an agitated state. "John, why did you take so long? The other boys have been back for a long time."

John held out his hands. "I am sorry, Master Ben. The net tangled many times as we pulled it in."

Master Ben grabbed John's arm tightly. "Hurry and finish collecting the fish and get back out on the lake."

John had lied for me. My weakness and constant sitting down kept us out on the lake too long. I did my best to keep up with John as we worked late into the evening. Pulling in nets. Bailing out water. Rowing. The same hard work over and over.

We ate a small portion of banku for dinner and a mat on the floor served as our bed. No real bed, money, or restaurant as Simon had promised.

Five of us boys shared one room. We could hardly turn over without bumping into someone else.

"Prince, do you think Mr Simon will be back in the morning to take us home?" I asked.

"Ha, ha." Another boy, Lionel, let out a laugh. "Are you stupid? He won't be back. He sold you to Master Ben."

"Sold?" I said, standing up. "He did not sell me. No one owns me."

Prince looked at me, possibly amazed at my forthrightness.

I began to walk towards the doorway. "I will tell Master Ben right now."

John grabbed my arm. "Shh. It is true, Kwaku. Master owns all of us. We are his property."

I pulled my arm away. "How can he own a person?"

"Did Master Ben give this man money?" Lionel said.

"Yes," Prince said. "He gave Simon money and said something like 'see how strong these boys are.'"

"Ha. That is it," Lionel said. "He sold you to Master Ben. Sit down and be quiet, Kwaku. Do you think you are special?"

I stared at Lionel with hate. He had nothing to do with selling me, but he seemed so uncaring. Almost mocking. He stood as tall as me and seemed about the same age. His right eye stayed white all the time—no pupil. Sort of deformed. I already disliked him.

John, on the other hand, offered a more consoling tone. "I'm sorry this happened to you both. All you can do now is work hard."

I laid my head down next to Prince and he stared back. A single tear rolled down his face.

* * *

Master Ben came in our room kicking our feet. "Get up, boys. Time to work." He allowed us no breakfast and pushed us out the door. "Go, go."

We paddled into the darkness. I joined John in the same boat as the day before.

"What time is it, John?"

"I do not know. About four hours until daylight. That is what time we start every day."

"Every day?"

"Sometimes we have Sunday off."

The smallest boy, William, joined us in the boat that day. Too weak to pull in the nets, he worked at bailing water out of the boat as we paddled. A seemingly endless task.

"William, how old are you?"

John chuckled. "He does not speak very much. He's only five. My little brother."

"How did you both come here?"

"So many questions, Kwaku," John said rolling his eyes. "We have been here two years. My father and mother died when I was little and William was an infant. We went to live with my grandparents for some time, but they were old and could not feed us. Master Ben said he would take care of us so they let him take us. William cried a lot so Master beat him. William stopped crying and rarely makes any noise now."

"Can he talk?"

William looked at John with a puzzled look. "Yes, he can, but he's afraid," John said.

My mind wandered and I stopped rowing. "Kwaku, why did you stop? Keep working. We will get in trouble."

"Sorry. I was thinking about Lionel. What is wrong with his eye? Why is it all white?"

John pointed to some limbs sticking out of the water. "You see these trees? They are everywhere. When you jump in the water, they can stab you. That is what happened to Lionel. He jumped in to untangle a net and a tree poked his eye. Now his eye is dead."

I looked back at John in horror. "Is that why he is so mean?"

"I don't know. I think he is mean because he hates being a slave. That is why he told you to sit down and be quiet. He was tricked into coming here like you."

"By Simon at Agbogbloshi?"

"No, Kwaku. Worse. His own mother. She told him he would work for one week and then she would be back for him. That was over a year ago. We are all mad about our condition, Kwaku. But what can we do? We can only work hard for our master and be smart so we are not punished. He will punish you, Kwaku."

"I will not let him. If he tries to beat me, I will fight back."

"No, Kwaku. He will only beat you worse. He is strong. Do not test him. I have seen him do mean things. Terrible things."

We returned to the shore and Master Ben allowed us a short time of rest. A girl waved us over to the shanty and served us porridge and cocoa. "What is your name, new boy?" she asked.

"I am Kwaku."

"I am Ivy," she said with a hint of a smile. She immediately reminded me of my sister Mercy and seemed the same age. Ivy worked with focus and determination. "Here, put these in your pocket. It is gari for you to eat on the lake."

"Thank you." In my exhaustion and in my terrible predicament, this small act of kindness revived me. I stood up straight and smiled back.

Slap!

A wave of pain ran through my body. My porridge and cocoa fell to the ground.

"You do not smile at her like that." Master Ben stooped and wagged his finger in my face.

I looked back at him, indignantly. My fists clenched up.

He noticed this. "Do you think you will fight back?"

Slap!

"Answer me. Do you think you will fight me?"

Tears streamed down my face, but I maintained my stare.

Slap!

The third slap knocked me to the ground. I sprang back up. "I want to leave this place."

"Ha. I own you now. You cannot leave. You can never leave. You work for me." Master held up his hand for another slap.

Although in tears, the sting of the slaps failed to stop my defiance.

"Ben!" A woman a few shanties over called for Master.

"Ahhh. Stupid boy," Master Ben said, and then walked away. Ivy retreated inside the shanty. The other boys looked at me with wide-open eyes.

John grabbed my arm. "Come, Kwaku." We sat under the tree and John shared his porridge and cocoa with me. "I told you not to test him. Do not stare at him. And do not talk to Ivy very much. Never smile at her."

"Why can I not talk to Ivy or smile at her?"

"Master Ben owns her."

"What do you mean?"

"You are stupid, Kwaku," Lionel said. "She is a slave like us. She does the housework. The cooking." Lionel smiled. "And sometimes she sleeps with Master."

"She is too young to be his wife. Why would she sleep with him?" I looked at Lionel for the answer to my question. Prince looked at Lionel. John looked at Lionel.

That is the moment I had my first lesson in sex education. I could tell by Prince's wide-open mouth, it was his first lesson as well. Lionel seemed to enjoy telling us about these very inappropriate things. Little William—oblivious to our conversation—played with a stick in the dirt.

"Lionel, you shouldn't be talking about this," John said.

"Why not? These boys need to learn. They have no father to teach them. They need to know how things in the world work."

For once in my life, I held back my questions. I had many, but feared the answers. I could not understand why Master Ben demanded this of Ivy.

"What if Ivy refuses?" Prince asked.

Lionel's lower jaw dropped. "Are you joking, Prince? You must be stupid. Of course she cannot refuse. He will beat her."

"She refused once," John said. "About one year ago."

We all turned our attention to John. Even little William stopped his artwork in the dirt and looked up.

"Master Ben had been drinking. He yelled at us for not working hard that day and told us to go to sleep. He threatened to beat us if we worked poorly the next day. Ivy started to lie on her mat when Master told her to come to his room. She looked up and said, 'No.' Master Ben grabbed her and dragged her into his room. She kicked at him and screamed." John stopped talking and looked out at the lake.

"What happened next?" Prince asked.

John looked back. "What do you think? Master came out of his room for his cane. I heard the beating. The whipping sound. Ivy screamed and cried. She begged Master to stop. This went on for twenty minutes. Ivy finally came out of the room, her clothes barely on. She looked at me, her lip bloody and right eye swollen shut. When she knelt down to her mat, I could see her back with red welts and blood oozing out. I tried to talk to her, but she pushed me away and said 'Don't touch me.'" John looked back at the lake. "Ivy has never refused him since."

John embodied strong character despite his enslavement, while Prince and I acted immaturely. Lionel bullied. But John dealt with it well. Not in any way happy, but he seemed to accept his condition. He was a fishing slave and he had to work. He spoke so matter-of-factly about things. But not with the story of Ivy. He looked so sad after he told it—as if it happened to him.

It occurred to me at this point that what Master Ben forced Ivy to do must have been the work my sister Mercy did late into the night. The thought gave me a burning sensation in my stomach. I knew I had to find a way to escape and rescue her.

SIX

One day Master Ben woke us and said, "John, come with me to the city. We have errands to do. William will stay with Ivy. Lionel, you will take Prince and Kwaku. Since there are three of you, I expect more work from that one boat. Understand?"

I had worked with Lionel once before but never without John. Lionel did not intimidate me physically, but he would be quick to tell Master if I did not obey him. Prince had learned to obey Lionel without opposition.

We barely left the shore and Lionel started talking. "We will catch many fish for Master today. We will work hard, boys. Hopefully, no one will drown." Lionel smiled.

Prince and I looked up. "What do you mean drown?" I said.

"Boys drown all the time. You must be a good swimmer in these waters." Lionel kept smiling. "Both of you can swim, right?"

"I can swim," Prince said. "You have seen me swim."

I remained silent.

Lionel leaned over to look around Prince who sat in the middle. "What about you, Kwaku? Can you swim?"

I slowly shook my head. "No. I have never learned."

I told John the same thing, and he said he would teach me soon, but he always jumped in the water to untangle the net so we could hurry home. The water terrified me. I could only see a few inches into the water and feared what might be lurking below.

"I will teach you today, Kwaku. You will be a good swimmer like me and Prince," Lionel said. "Let's just hope there are no crocodiles."

Prince looked up. "There are no crocodiles."

"There are," Lionel said. "There are crocodiles and electric fish."

"You are lying." Prince continued to argue with Lionel while I remained silent, pretending not to listen.

"Ask anyone. I have seen them myself. Huge crocodiles. As long as this boat. They can swallow a boy whole. They wait until you dive in to untangle the net. Then they attack!" Lionel clapped his arms closed to simulate a crocodile.

"I don't believe you. And what do you mean electric fish? There's no such thing."

"There are electric fish. There are eels. Very long, like a giant worm. They rub against you and shock you and paralyse you so you cannot swim and you drown. This happens."

"All lies."

"You ask John. He will tell you."

I listened to this back and forth between them, my heart racing. I resolved that I would not go in. No matter what. My job was in the boat. Lionel had to be lying, anyway. Electric fish. Crocodiles. Ha, I thought. He only wanted to scare us.

We reached one net after daybreak—full of fish. We pulled and pulled, labouring over the heavy catch. After several weeks of fishing, the sore muscles subsided, but I certainly continued to struggle with the constant physical demands. Master Ben gave us a short break most afternoons and a few hours to sleep at night. But most of the time, we worked. One day I even prayed that God would take away all of the fish from the lake so we would not have to work. My hands—cut and blistered the first week—had began to toughen with calluses.

I noticed that Prince began developing muscles in his upper body like those of John and Lionel. It seemed unnatural. A boy should not have huge shoulder and chest muscles.

My feet remained sore from constant immersion in water. The boat never dried. These conditions, coupled with a poor diet, were simply inhumane.

"Pull harder," Lionel said. "Pull."

Suddenly, we could no longer pull. The net had caught on something under water. The moment I had feared arrived. Someone needed to dive in and untangle the net. Since Master Ben told us to bring in more fish than normal, maybe Lionel would dive in and quickly untangle the net so we could hurry. Or perhaps he would tell Prince to do it, since he could already swim. We did not have time for a swimming lesson. Yes, I thought, I would be spared this time.

"The net is tangled," Lionel said. "Kwaku, go untangle it."

"But . . . but, I cannot swim."

"You must learn."

"No, I will go. I want to go," Prince said, pointing his thumb to his chest.

We both knew that Lionel just wanted to force me in the water. He was a bully and that is what bullies do.

"No. I am in charge." Lionel stood and began wagging his finger. "Master Ben leaves these decisions to me. Kwaku, you must learn. Jump in and untangle the net."

I looked at the water on both sides of the boat. Anything I could do to stall. Lionel grabbed some rope. "Tie this around your ankle. If you don't come up soon, we will pull you up."

I tied the rope around my ankle as tight as possible. Leaning over the water, I determined to delay the inevitable as long as possible. I looked at Prince who had no response. As I leaned over the edge of the boat trying to see beneath the surface, Lionel pushed me in. A gulp of lakewater filled my mouth and I managed to kick my way back to the boat and held on. Lionel laughed.

"Wave your arms in the water and kick your feet. Relax your body," Prince said.

Lionel continued his mocking. "Swim, Kwaku. Swim. Ha, ha."

Gulp! "Help!" I bobbed up and down several times.

"What kind of boy cannot swim?" Lionel asked, pushing my arms from the boat. "Swim down and untangle the net. Ha, ha. And watch out for crocodiles."

After a few minutes of splashing, sinking, coughing water, and grabbing the boat, I managed to make my way a short distance and back, without going under. The net served as a lifeline to guide me, and I quickly learned to hold my breath under water. I followed the net down and noticed it wrapped around tree limbs. Fish caught in the net stared back at me. Their helpless look of imprisonment mirrored my own. After several seconds of untangling, the net barely released, so I swam to the surface for air.

"What is taking so long, Kwaku?" Lionel said. "We do not have all day. Master Ben will punish us if we do not hurry."

Breathing heavily, I grabbed the side of the boat to rest. "It is very tangled. I am not sure if I can get it loose."

Lionel pushed my hand away from the boat. "Try harder. Go back down." He shook his head in disgust. "And don't touch the electric fish. Ha, ha."

Prince nodded. "You can do this, Kwaku."

My swimming skills still lacked much practice, but I felt some confidence at going under water with the net as my guide. I took a deep breath and headed down. The rope around my ankle gave me some comfort, although I did not know how long they would wait to pull me up. The visibility only allowed me to see a few feet. I found the place of the main tangle and went to work on that.

As it loosened, the portion of the net that had been held in tension sprang across my body and wrapped around me. Now the net caught me. Panicking, I opened my mouth and it filled with water. Several fish escaped through a hole in the net and swam past me. I worked furiously with my hands to untangle myself, but nothing worked. I felt a sharp pull at my ankle where the rope attached. Lionel and Prince must have thought I had been under for too long. They pulled me towards the surface but the net kept me under. I gulped and bubbles surrounded me. Now upside down, water filled my nostrils causing a burning sensation.

My life would end this way? Not crocodiles. Not electric fish. But drowning?

An enormous pressure squeezed my head and I felt exhausted from the struggle. My eyes stung and everything seemed blurry. A rope pulling my ankle to the surface and the net holding me under.

In that instant, several images ran through my head. My father walking out the door the day he died. My mother staring out the window. My sister Mercy struggling with Auntie Agnes. Where are you, Mercy? I had lost everything but now felt more helpless than ever.

Then the net loosened all around me. I was free. Someone pulled at my arm and I broke through the surface to fresh air. I coughed and spit out water. Prince floated next to me.

"Are you alright?" He pulled me towards the boat.

I did not know what to say or feel. In mere seconds, I went from death to life. Prince saved me that day. A true hero. A true friend. I looked back at him in disbelief, knowing I would thank him many times over the next several days. Prince would likely have an easier life without the burden of taking care of me.

Lionel offered no consolation. Just more mocking. "Kwaku, you are so stupid. You almost drowned. What kind of fisherman are you?"

With the net loosened, we pulled it in and returned to shore. Master Ben warned us about taking too long to come back. I knew Lionel would make some excuse if needed rather than tell him he had wasted time teaching me to swim, but the large catch seemed to please Master Ben.

I had experienced so many traumatic events in the last several weeks, but the feeling of drowing in those murky waters disturbed me the most. I resolved that I must remove myself from this dangerous situation. I resolved to be free. I had to escape.

* * *

Devising an escape plan proved difficult. Who to include became my first problem. I did not trust Lionel, and since he slept in the same room as us, we could not discuss this issue at night. Besides, Master Ben might be listening. Master watched Ivy closely and any long conversation with her might arouse suspicion. Little William never talked, but in the event that he did, he might accidentally divulge the plan. Sometimes Master let us rest on Sunday and we would play football in the lot. However, Lionel always played with us.

The morning Lionel woke up sick, gave us an opportunity. Master Ben usually made us work when we were sick, but Lionel's vomiting convinced Master that he would only be a hindrance in the boat. Master sent John, Prince, and me out—leaving William with Ivy. We pushed off and just before we reached the first net, I offered up my plan. In reality, I had no plan—only a wish.

"Listen, I am going to escape and I want you both to come with me."

Prince and John both stopped rowing and looked at me.

"Are you crazy?" Prince said.

"Shh." I held up my finger to my mouth. "You are too loud. Your voice carries over the water."

"He isn't crazy, Prince," John said, surprising me, and from Prince's puzzled stare, surprised him as well. "Boys have run away before. Not from Master Ben, but I have heard of it."

"How did they get away?" I asked.

John grabbed the net. "Listen, we must keep doing our work. We can talk as we paddle back and forth. We must not say anything to Lionel. He will tell Master if he finds out."

We kept working as John continued. "The boys that escape always go in the night when it is dark and their Master is asleep. They try and get on a *trotro* bus or hide on some truck."

"What else?" I said.

"That's all I know. I have only heard of it happening."

"We cannot go at night," I said. "Lionel will wake up or Master Ben will hear us opening the door."

Prince held up his finger. "I have an idea. We could get Ivy to distract Lionel and Master Ben somehow."

"But Ivy will come with us. We will all run away," I said.

"She is a girl. She will slow us down," Prince said.

I stopped paddling to make my protest. "How do you know this? She can run as fast as we can. You have seen her play football with us. No, everyone will be included except Lionel."

"Keep paddling," John said. "Now listen. I cannot go because of William."

"Why?" I said. "We have seen him run. He is fast and strong. He will make it."

"No. It's not that. What if we are caught? Do you understand the beating Master Ben will give us? I saw what he did to Ivy just for saying 'no.' I would risk the beating, but I am afraid of what he would do to William. I cannot risk that. I will help you, but I will not go."

The possibility of punishment had not occurred to me until now. I knew there would be risk, but the thought of a beating gave me pause. Prince felt no trepidation.

"I'm not afraid of a beating. He can catch me and beat me and I will run away again."

I sat up straight and pointed my thumb to my chest. "Me, too," I said.

Our escape discussion continued through the morning. As dawn turned the surface of the lake red, we ventured to our farthest net. After pulling it in with our catch, Prince and I began to paddle but John sat still in the boat looking towards the shore.

"I have an idea."

We both stopped our paddling and leaned towards John.

"You see that village. That is where Master Ben has taken us a few times to buy food and supplies. It is much larger than our village and I have seen *trotro* buses stop there. That is where you will make your escape. Our village is small and so are the ones near us. There are no trucks or *trotros*."

For the first time that morning, I got excited that it might happen. John's idea seemed to have so much promise. Prince quickly took away my excitement.

"John, how do we get there? If we sneak out, we cannot walk on water. We cannot drive. That is too far to walk. It must be 30 kilometres to get there."

John smiled. "You will take a boat." He looked at us with a wide smile. "We must get back. I will tell you as we paddle. You will sneak Ivy into the boat late at night and paddle to this side of the lake. You must turn the boat over and swim part of the way. Master will know you escaped, but think you drowned. When you get to the village, you wait until morning and sneak on to the *trotro* or find some other way to go to Accra. What do you think?"

"It is a good plan," I said. "What do you think, Prince?"

"It's good, but how will we sneak out?"

"I have an idea for that," John said. "We will wait until a night when Master Ben is drinking. He will walk off with his friends, but not before I convince him that you two need to learn to work on your own. Lionel will go in the boat with me and I will take William. Ivy can go with you. I will convince Master to go to bed and that I will wait for you to come in. He never cares on nights he drinks. He will expect you to take longer since Lionel and I are not

50

leading you. I will say the same to Lionel. Since it was my idea, I should be the one to wait up for you. That way, you will not even need to sneak the boat out."

"But what if Master Ben wants Ivy to sleep with him?" Prince asked.

John looked up in the air for another idea. "She will pretend to be very sick. Like she's about to vomit. Master will leave her alone. I will tell Ivy later. I will find a time to tell her the plan."

My smile grew larger. This seemed like a great plan. "John, I am worried you will get in trouble."

"Master will never know it was me. I will tell him that it is my fault. That I suggested you go out, but he will not know I was helping you escape. He will think you drowned. Lionel will say that I was in the boat with him. I will tell him that I don't know what happened to Ivy."

For boys our age, this plan, however misguided, seemed foolproof. What could go wrong?

SEVEN

"Ivy, we must go now." Prince waved from the shore for us to hurry to the boat. John, William, and Lionel had already paddled far away but not before Lionel mocked us for taking so long.

Ivy held on to the shanty doorframe as if about to fall off a ledge. "No, Kwaku. I cannot go. I'm scared. Master will beat me if we are caught. He will beat us all."

"I know you are scared. But we must run away from this place. From Master Ben."

"No, I will slow you down. You must go fast."

"I have seen you run, Ivy. You are as fast as both of us. Please, come with us."

"Kwaku. Go." She placed her hands on my shoulder and looked into my eyes. "Good luck."

I knew further pleadings would be useless and headed towards the boat.

"Kwaku, wait." Ivy ran into the shanty and came back clutching something in her hand. "Here. Take it. I know where Master hides his money. You can use this for the *trotro* or food or whatever you need."

"No, Ivy. You will get in trouble."

"It is not that much. He may not even notice. Now go."

I ran to the boat and pushed out. Prince paddled furiously. We had plenty of time once on the water but we wanted to get away from shore before Master returned. We hoped John could cover for our absence at least until morning. John planned to tell Master about Lionel forcing me in the water. He would say that our net probably got caught, and we both drowned trying to free it.

"I will not let him beat us, Kwaku."

"What do you mean?"

"If Master catches us, I will fight him." Prince held both fists clenched like a boxer.

"He is strong, Prince."

"Not if we fight him together. We can defeat him."

"Let us hope we do not have to. Paddle. We need to get to the other shore."

Unfortunately, the weather did not comply with our escape plan. The wind blew harder than normal that night, creating large waves. We paddled hard but felt as though we went back a little for every movement forward. The crescent moon offered little light. We used a few small islands John showed us as our guide and paddled for hours until we saw the other shore. During the day, everyone could see the village that lay near the top of the hill, but at night, the darkness obscured it. John had shown us a huge tree that grew straight out of a cliff for our marker. We planned to leave the boat near there for our drowning ruse and swim to the shore just right of that cliff. With cliffs to our left and the vastness of the lake to our right, we intended to navigate our way to the village only a few kilometres or so from there.

I had practised my swimming some in the days leading up to the escape. Far from proficient, I felt both confident and motivated enough to make the swim to shore.

Prince stopped paddling. I followed suit and we drifted slowly. He pointed to the tree protruding from the cliff. Enough moonlight glistened off the rockface to see the tree.

"This is the spot. Let's go."

We both hung our feet over the side of the boat, grabbing the other end. We then pulled with all of our might, tipping the boat over. We thought this might make the story of a terrible boat accident even more convincing. The net sank and the oars floated away. We swam furiously. The shore looked so close when we were in the boat, but now seemed far away. Fishing had made me strong, but I quickly felt weakened. We had already exhausted ourselves from the paddling.

"Prince, wait. I need to rest."

"We're almost there. Keep swimming."

My swimming strokes reduced to slow lurches towards the shore. Every muscle in my body screamed for rest. The minutes seemed like hours. While I should have focused on the escape plan, delirious thoughts filled my head. Thoughts that seemed more like a dream. I thought of riding a white horse into battle with a sword at my side. I had no control over the horse. It led the way. It knew where the battle lay. I held on tightly, a willing accomplice. I lost myself in this daydream. Then I lost Prince.

Where's Prince? I splashed and turned around. "Prince! Prince, where are you?"

"Shh. Kwaku, be quiet. Stand up."

I extended my legs and felt the soft sand. I stood and the water reached only to my waist. In my state of mixed exhaustion and frenzy, I had managed to make shore and felt a little silly that I panicked.

Prince, completely focused, surveyed each direction. "Come, Kwaku, we must rest, dry our clothes, and then get to the village."

We moved to an area with several trees. I took off my shirt, wrung out the water, and hung it on a limb. I did the same with my pants and realised I had made a grave mistake. The money. The cedis Ivy gave me survived the swim but were all wet.

"Prince, look at the money."

"That's OK, Kwaku. We will lay them out. People should understand wet money in a fishing village. They will be dry enough."

We sat there, naked and alone in the darkness for one hour. The rest felt good, but my thirst grew stronger by the minute. All that water around, but I did not dare drink from it. Nearly every time someone did drink from the lake, they got sick. We had money. We could buy something to drink later.

My heavy eyelids began to close; my body was desperate for sleep.

Prince stood up and felt his clothes. "It is time. We must go now."

Our clothes remained damp, but we always wore wet clothes. The money, also wet, dried enough that it did not tear.

"Prince, we should divide the money in half, in case we are separated."

The thought of being separated from Prince terrified me. However, I wanted him to make it if I could not. If anyone could escape, Prince could. He eclipsed me in every way—in mind, body, and will.

"If only one of us makes it, we should find help for the rest. For John and William and Ivy," I said.

"What about Lionel?" Prince asked.

"What about him? Who cares about him?"

"I don't like him either. But maybe he's so mean because he is a slave. Because his mother abandoned him. No one should be a slave."

"Sorrow for Lionel? The one who mocked me. The one who almost drowned me." However, the one who was a slave like me, I thought. "I guess so, Prince. I guess we all deserve our freedom."

We ran some and walked some. As the sun began to rise, we saw the village up ahead. We approached a group of buildings on the outskirts and looked over the area. I shivered.

Prince placed his hand on my shoulder. "What's wrong? Why are you shaking?"

"I am cold from the wet clothes." I lied.

Our clothes had nearly dried. I quivered from fear. The whole experience scared me and now we had to face other people.

"We must blend in. We must act as if we live here. It is a big village. People will think we're just regular children," Prince said.

People bustled about performing their morning routines. A girl in her brown and yellow school uniform fetched water. She must have awakened early for chores but then would enjoy a day's learning. She looked content. I longed for her life. Several men gathered around the engine of an old car arguing over how to fix it. The smell of baking bread made me hungry.

I thought of my mummy and her tea bread. Mummy's tea bread was the best anyone could eat. I missed her so much. I missed her, as well as Father and Mercy. Simon had taken us seven or eight weeks earlier. Mercy had to be so worried about me. I wondered what she might be doing.

Prince pulled the cedis from his pocket and looked at me. "Let's buy something to eat."

"What about the *trotro*? How much is that?" I said, pulling my money out and counting it.

"I will go ask someone where we board the bus and the amount of the fare. You stay here. We do not want to look suspicious."

Prince jumped up and approached some women with head trays. For a long time the ladies talked to each other and pointed. They finally nodded and Prince ran back to me with some tea bread.

"What did they say?"

"We must walk down this road for about thirty minutes. They think the *trotro* bus to Accra leaves in two hours. The fare is not much so I bought us some bread."

"What about something to drink? I am so thirsty."

"C'mon, Kwaku. We can find some running water on the way."

We headed down the road. My empty stomach craved the bread but it did not taste near as good as Mummy's bread. Within five minutes, we found a water faucet and drank our fill. I felt renewed. We had made it so far. By afternoon we might be in Accra. We might even make it to Agbogbloshie. Prince could go home, and I could find Mercy. I became excited over the thought.

We walked briskly, but not too fast. I felt as though everyone stared at me. As if, they all knew. "Prince, do you think these people know we escaped?"

"How could they know? Don't worry about that. But, we cannot trust them. You saw all the fishing boats. Fishermen stick together. We cannot ask for help. They will send us back to Master Ben."

"What if we tell a policeman?"

"No, Kwaku. We cannot trust anyone. We must stay with the plan."

We asked for directions again and after walking for nearly one hour, we saw several *trotros* parked off to the side of a busy intersection. Many of them had different locations on signs in the front windows. Some names we knew, some we did not. We did not see "Accra".

Prince approached one of the drivers at their window. "Sir, where is the *trotro* to Accra?

"It's not here yet. Maybe in thirty minutes." He quickly dismissed us and drove off.

We could think of nothing else to do. We had schemed, paddled, swam, ran, and now we waited. Waited for the *trotro* ride to freedom. Our wait seemed much longer than thirty minutes, when a yellow *trotro* with the word ACCRA in the front window drove right past us. We panicked for a brief moment, but it eventually stopped. The words IN GOD WE TRUST emblazoned the back window. We put our arms around each other, ran towards the *trotro*, and got in line behind others about to board.

John's great plan had worked. A man behind us complained about waiting to board. He wore a suit and carried a briefcase. An important businessman perhaps. Maybe I would be like him one day. We kept looking at one another and smiled as the line inched towards the door to board. We both grasped our cedis ready to pay the fare. A baby, strapped to its mummy's back, turned and looked at us with a hint of a smile. So cute. So innocent.

Prince looked at me. "Almost home, Kwaku."

For the first time in a long time, I felt my luck had changed.

"Hello, boys."

The voice behind us could only belong to one person. I am embarrassed to say that urine ran down my leg at the sound.

Prince and I turned at the same time. Master Ben stood there, arms folded and grinning. His smile could not hide the evil in his eyes. They pierced through me.

"You foolish boys." He spoke quietly. "You think you could escape from me." He grabbed both of our arms.

I thought of screaming for help but remembered Prince's words that fishermen stick together. I felt helpless and complied. Prince fought him some but Master ignored his kicks and pleas, dragging him to the car.

A few people looked, but did nothing. Master's friend from the village stood by a car, opening the door. Master threw us in the back seat and sat next to us. The other man got in front and drove off.

"You boys are stupid. Don't you understand? I own you. I paid for you. You cannot simply run off."

Prince continued to struggle and thrust his elbow striking Master in the side. Master slapped him across the face. Prince fell towards me and ended his resistance.

Master continued his lecture. "I see everything. I know everything. You will never leave me. You should be fishing right now but are wasting time. Losing my money."

Master smacked the back of my head. "Where is my boat, huh?"

I looked at him but gave no response. Prince remained silent.

Master looked right into my eyes. "You will pay for this." I knew this meant severe punishment and feared the inevitable.

The car ride seemed an eternity. We arrived at the little village much the same as when Simon had delivered us to our prison.

Master held open the door. "Get out, boys. Come."

We walked towards the shanty. I saw Ivy first. She looked at us with deep sorrow. I could tell she had been crying. John and Lionel pulled at a net near the shore with little William trying to help.

Master called to them. "You boys, come here." Master stormed into the shanty and returned with a cane. "I own all of you. You must obey me or be punished."

Then he looked directly at me. "I know, Kwaku. I know this was all your idea."

I shook my head. "No, sir. No." I lied.

It was my idea. Our beatings would be my fault. Master grabbed my arm and bent me over the old boat that rested upside down near the shanty. It had so many holes that it would sink in seconds.

Whap!

The first strike of the cane sent searing pain throughout my body. I had never felt such agony. I tried to scream. My mouth opened, but no noise came out. I could not breathe.

I looked over at the others in desperation. Little William wept, hugging John's leg.

Ivy cried and I could see her mouthing the word "no," over and over.

Then I saw Lionel. No tears for him. Only a huge grin. He actually enjoyed this. I could not see Prince, though.

"This will be a lesson to all of you," Master Ben said.

Whap!

"Ahhh!" My voice returned with a loud cry. The second one hurt worse than the first. I felt a wetness on my buttocks. Blood, perhaps. I tried to get up, but Master held me down with his foot on my back.

How many strokes of the cane? How many of these?

Whap!

I looked up to see Master with the cane raised for a fourth swing when another body came into view. Prince tackled Master Ben. The cane flew out of his hands. I pulled myself up from the boat in disbelief. Prince began wildly swinging at Master, landing several blows. Master kicked him off and Prince rolled away.

Prince screamed, "I hate you! You don't own me! I hate you! I hate you!"

Master picked up an old paddle that lay near. Prince charged him but Master stepped aside and pushed him down.

"Stop it, you stupid boy! Stop it."

Prince jumped up and charged him again. "I hate you!"

Master swung the paddle striking Prince in the head.

Thud.

Prince fell to the ground and lay motionless. Blood oozed from his temple.

Master yelled. "Get up. Get up, you stupid boy."

Prince didn't reply. He didn't move. Lifeless. Master leaned down to feel him.

He looked at me. "You see what you've done, Kwaku? You killed him. This is your fault. Do you know how much he cost me?"

Master threw the oar down. He looked around for several seconds. Was he thinking about what he had done? Was he looking to see if anyone had witnessed this? Would he return to my caning?

"Lionel. Grab his feet."

Master grabbed Prince under the shoulders while Lionel struggled to pick him up under his heels. They walked over to a boat by the shore and set Prince down in the boat. Master used a knife to cut a section of old netting and loaded some rocks into the boat. Master and Lionel stepped in the boat with Prince's body and paddled away.

Master Ben left no instructions with us. We stood there. Helpless. Confused. Lost.

"This is our fault, Kwaku," Ivy said, tears streaming down her cheeks.

I looked at her and cocked my head. "How is this your fault?"

"No, Ivy. I will tell him," John said. "William, go over there and play." William ran off to the big tree and played in the dirt. His innocence did not know how to process this. Playing likely seemed a good option.

I rubbed my bottom. I had felt inside my pants at the small amount of blood that had not soaked into them.

John turned away from me and rubbed the sides of his head. He turned back wiping his eyes.

"Listen, Kwaku. Last night, after we returned from fishing, I thought Lionel had walked away from the shanty. Master had not yet returned from drinking. Ivy and me...we—" John looked down at the ground. "We started talking about the escape plan. About you leaving the boat in the water. About the big village. About the *trotro* to Accra. We were so excited for you." John looked directly at me. "Lionel heard everything. He was standing right outside and we didn't know it. As soon as Master Ben returned, he told him everything. Master went into a rage. He slapped me and started to slap Ivy, but then stopped and said we would have to watch you and Prince's punishment before receiving ours."

The searing pain on my buttocks subsided, thinking about Prince.

Ivy walked over and hugged me. "I am so sorry, Kwaku."

I looked at John and Ivy. "This is not your fault. This is Lionel. I will make him pay for this. I will beat Lionel for this."

"No," John said. "No more of that. No more fighting."

* * *

We saw Master and Lionel returning an hour later. While they paddled to shore, we pondered our fate.

I rubbed my bottom. "Will he cane me more?"

"He might beat all of us," John said. "Not William, though. He cannot be mad at him. I cannot let him beat William."

Ivy placed her hands on William's shoulders. "We will all protect William. No matter the cost."

Master said something to Lionel out of earshot. He shook his finger at him and Lionel nodded. We stood together. Resolute. Ready to face what came. Running away seemed fruitless. We had no place to hide. I glanced down near the old boat where Master beat me. A small puddle of blood remained where Prince died.

Master walked up. "John, you and Kwaku take the boat and bring in the nets." Then he walked away. So matter-of-fact. No emotion. No rage. Just his typical voice he used to give us orders.

Ivy grabbed William's hand and took him in the shanty.

I took one step towards the boat and looked at Lionel. No grin. No joy. No mocking. His lower lip stuck out and slightly quivered. Tears fell down his cheek. He opened his mouth to speak but no words came out. Lionel had changed on that boat ride. All his confidence and arrogance left him. He never wanted Prince to die.

Slaves. That is all we were. No one to protect us. No one to help us. We fished. That is all we could do.

EIGHT

A full year passed since Prince's death. I stood in the boat, net in hands and looked over the water. The ripples barely rocked the boat. Although land surrounded me, there remained parts of the lake where I could not see land. Only a small portion where the water met the sky. That seemed magical to me. Sometimes I thought that if I paddled towards that point, I would find a new life. That was my dream. A new life. A free person. A mum and father. Siblings. Friends. School. A Football star. I dreamed of a different life.

"Kwaku, what are you doing? Pull," Lionel said.

I typically fished with Lionel now. His bullying and hatred ended the day Master killed Prince. Wrapping Prince's body in a fishing net with rocks and dumping him in the water had done it. Seeing Prince's face staring back at him as his body sank haunted him. He told me once about all of it but refused to discuss it anymore. Lionel and I were not friends. Just co-workers. Fellow slaves.

William, still a young boy of about six or seven, worked in the other boat with John. Ivy still cooked our meals, cleaned the shanty, and succumbed to Master's urges on occasion. I hated that more than anything. I hated Master for killing Prince and enslaving us, and my anger renewed whenever he forced Ivy into his bed.

As Lionel and I returned with the final catch of the day, my mood improved knowing that the next day was Sunday, and we would play football.

Several months before, Master had allowed us to rest every Sunday and we used that time to run around the village or play football. I do not think he did this out of kindness, but rather because he drank late on Saturday nights and did not want to supervise us on Sunday. Perhaps he needed the day off.

A couple of older boys in the village began teaching me the finer points of the game and helped me hone my technique. The sport came to me naturally. I had no problem dribbling around most defenders, but my greatest talent proved in kicking the ball exactly where I wanted it to go. I think playing in bare feet provided a certain feel for the ball that other players lacked. We had no football pitch—just a large space of dirt where we could play. We used a tree and a large rock for one goal. The bumper-to-bumper length of an old rusted car represented the other goal. My favourite trick involved shooting the ball in the rear window of the old car where the glass had broken out. Even at a distance of thirty metres, I hit the target consistently.

I loved football, but I remained a slave. We still awoke at 4.00 a.m. to retrieve the nets. We still worked hard all day. Master continued sending us out in the evening to set more nets. We constantly mended torn nets and pulled out tiny dead fish and twigs. Six days a week, we laboured for

16 or 17 hours per day. While the hard work taxed us, the monotony could be maddening. We endured the stroke of the cane on occasion.

* * *

"John, pass!"

I raised my hand while running to show John that I had perfect position to score a goal. John sent the ball my way. Not a single blade of grass existed on our pitch. I kicked up dirt as I ran. Sweat poured off me. Without stopping the ball, I planted my left foot and shot it with the inside of my right foot—barely enough to change the momentum. The ball grazed the rock scoring a goal. My fellow teammates rejoiced with me. Six of us, all fisherboys in the village, playing six fisherboys on the other team.

One of the boys on my team patted me on the back. "You should come by my Master's shop. He will have the game on television."

"What game?" I asked.

He looked at me with his head cocked. "The African Cup. The Black Stars are playing Cameroon."

I had known of the Black Stars and of the African Cup. But my isolation kept me from any news. It kept me from knowing when the Black Stars played. That the African Cup of Nations had started.

We followed him to his master's shop where that master sold goods, in addition to forcing boys to fish. The television lit up with a huge antenna resting on top. Several men sat around watching, including Master Ben.

As we walked up, he turned and noticed John and me, but said nothing and turned back to the game.

The shop owner looked at us as well. "Ben, you have five boys, don't you?"

Master Ben, without even looking away from the television said, "No. I had five boys, but one drowned."

It did not surprise me that Master Ben would lie about killing Prince. I wanted desperately to scream out that Master murdered him, but I knew that would do no good. I turned my attention to the game.

Behind the several men who sat around the television, at least ten of us boys fought for a good position to see. I had seen football on television before. But now, I knew more about the game. I learned some of the skills they used. I watched the strategy of both teams. While others rejoiced when Ghana scored a goal, I evaluated the movements of the players to score the goal—how the play developed.

I had no real happiness as a fisherboy. I am sure my birthday came and went, but I had no idea when it occurred. My dream of a better life kept me going. Watching Ghana defeat Cameroon and advance in the tournament gave me some joy. It gave me some national pride to watch my team triumph. I rejoiced with my fellow fisherboys for our Black Stars as we began walking away from the shop. I continued thinking of my dream. The one where I play for the Black Stars and score a goal.

"Why are you boys so happy?" I turned to see a man smiling back at me in a dashiki suit.

I pointed towards the television. "The Black Stars just defeated Cameroon. They will advance in the African Cup."

"Ah. That is good news. That is worth rejoicing." He looked at each of us. "Tell me your name?"

I looked over both shoulders and stood alone as the other boys kept walking. "Uh. I am Kwaku."

"Hello, Kwaku, I am Paul. Paul Boateng. But you can call me Paul." He held out his hand. "It's good to meet you."

I extended my hand and we shook. "Who are you?"

"I'm glad you asked, Kwaku. I am from Accra but visit these little villages on occasion. Do you live here with your parents?"

I shook my head back and forth and pointed towards the television. "No, sir. I am a fisherboy. I work for Master Ben over there. The one in the red shirt."

"I see. Well, do you mind if we talk?"

"About what? Why are you here?"

Paul placed his hands behind his back and leaned towards me. "I am here for kingdom work." He spoke deliberately. No words wasted.

"Kingdom work? What is that?"

"Can we walk over there where it is more quiet, and I will tell you?" he said, extending his arm and leading the way. "Kwaku, I serve God in many ways. But one of them, and likely the most important way, is helping other people find peace with God."

"I know of God, sir. My father used to say, 'Always look for God,' whenever we faced a bad situation or were sad."

"Your father sounds like a wise man. What happened to him, if you don't mind me asking?"

"He was killed in a construction accident in Kumasi. My mum brought me and my sister to Accra to look for work and then my mum got sick and died in the guest home."

"And how did you end up in this village?"

"I got separated from my sister and a man brought me here and sold me to Master Ben. I have worked for him for about a year or so."

Paul placed his hands on my shoulders. "Kwaku, I cannot tell you how sorry I am for this. I am so sorry you have experienced this."

His head tilted slightly—focusing his eyes on me. He cared.

"Well, I really do not look for God anymore. I am sure he is out there, but I do not think he wants to help me."

"Oh, Kwaku. I can see why you would feel this way. But what if I told you that God is not only out there, but is all around us? And, he wants to help you."

"How can he help me?"

Paul laughed. "You ask very good questions, Kwaku. God wants to help you. He wants to help me. It's just that sometimes he helps us in ways we don't understand. Sometimes he allows us to go through things—difficult things—to teach us or to show us something."

Although I remained confused at much this stranger told me, I could not help but listen to every word. I wanted to know everything he had to say. "What is God showing me?"

"Kwaku, I cannot tell you for certain. I can tell you the most important thing that God wants you to know."

I stopped walking and looked directly at Paul. "What?"

"He wants peace with you. Peace through his son, Jesus Christ. Have you heard of Jesus?"

"Yes, sir. My father talked about him all the time, but I never really paid attention. My mum would always say, 'Oh, Jesus, help me,' when she was frustrated. But I do not believe God wants peace with me."

Paul leaned in. "Now why would you say that?"

"Letting my father get killed. Letting my mum get sick and die. Making me a slave. Making my sister…"

"Making your sister what?"

I looked away towards the lake. "I do not like to talk about it."

"Kwaku. I wish I could tell you why God allowed those things to happen. I wish I could give you a specific reason why these things happened to you and your family. What I can tell you is this. God allows these things to happen for his purposes."

I stood up. "No. This is not right. God does not work like that. That makes no sense. How can I find peace when I am a slave? Forced to fish all day. It was not very peaceful when Master caned me."

Paul stood up and placed a hand on my shoulder. "Listen, Kwaku. It isn't easy to understand. We will never know everything about God. We must have faith. It is faith that we must live by."

"But I do not see God doing anything for me."

"Have you talked with him?"

"With who?"

Paul laughed. "With God. You know. Do you pray?"

"Oh. Not that much. I prayed for my mum to get better, but it did not work."

Paul placed his other hand on my other shoulder and stared at me. "Keep praying. I assure you, God is listening. And he cares."

"Yeah!" I heard loud cheers coming from the football pitch.

"I have to go."

"I understand, Kwaku. Will you think about what I said?"

"Yes, sir."

"Kwaku, really think about this. Talk to God. I will be back next week. Maybe we can talk again."

* * *

The next Sunday we played football as usual. More and more boys came to play and even a few girls. One day we had enough for eight on one team and nine on the other. I gained more and more confidence at my ability to do anything I wanted with a football. Dribbling, passing, receiving, heading, and kicking. My teammates typically urged me to play the centre-forward position, but none of us did a very good job of holding our positions.

I loved it. Every minute of it.

We took a break at midday. Our pitch was in the middle of the village—near many shops. While drinking from the faucet, I noticed Mr Boateng talking with some children and an older girl. He noticed me and waved me over.

"I will be back later," I said to my teammates.

Paul met me halfway. "Hello, Kwaku. Do you remember me?"

"Yes, sir. Mr Boateng."

He offered me his hand to shake. "Remember, you may call me Paul."

"Paul, who is that?" I said, pointing to the older girl talking with the children.

She seemed much more well dressed than other girls in the village.

"My daughter Bridget." He motioned for her to come over. "Bridget, this is Kwaku. The one I told you about."

"Good to meet you, Kwaku. I watched you play football. You are very talented. You must have been playing your whole life."

I pointed to my chest. "Me? No, I just started about a few months ago."

"Ah. Well, you must be a natural." She looked at the children and then looked back at Paul. "Daa, I must finish my lesson."

"Go ahead," Paul said.

"Does she do the kingdom work?"

Paul laughed. "Yes, she does the kingdom work. Can we sit and talk some more?"

"I guess so." I wanted to make sure I did not miss any football but felt compelled to talk to Paul. We walked over towards some large rocks and sat down.

"Did you think about our talk, Kwaku? And pray?"

"A little . . . well . . . not really."

"That's OK. Look over there and tell me what you see," Paul said, pointing across the lake.

I looked intently. "I see water. The same water I see every day."

"Yes. Now look farther."

"I see the hills."

"And what else. Name everything you see."

"I see the water, and hills, and sky, and trees, and people."

"Do you know what that is called, Kwaku? God's creation. It's all created for his pleasure and glory. Do you understand?"

"I think so."

"Is it fair that some water he makes clear and beautiful but some remains stagnant? Is it fair that he makes some hills tall and some short? Is it fair that he lets some trees live for hundreds of years and some he allows to be chopped down after only a few years?"

I paused for a moment thinking for a response. "I guess so."

"Kwaku, is it fair that some children grow up in grand homes with plenty of food and a good education while some grow up in poverty?"

"No, it is not fair."

"You are right, Kwaku. It's not fair. God is not about fairness. He is about his will. He is about his plan of redemption."

I cocked my head in confusion. "Rademp . . . "

"Redemption. It means restoring peace to a broken relationship. It means that we are all separated from God through our sins. He sent Jesus Christ to die on the cross to pay the price of our sins. To redeem us. When we trust in Jesus as our redeemer—our saviour—we have peace with God. We have eternal life."

I sat there listening. Last time Paul talked about God, it made me mad at what had happened in my life. Today seemed different. I became more curious. "My father talked about Jesus, but I never understood who he was."

"A great question, Kwaku. He is the son of God. The Bible says that God loved the world so much, he gave his only son, that whoever believes in him will not perish, but have eternal life. That is Jesus."

"Kwaku. Come on. Let's go," one of my teammates said from the football pitch.

I stood up. "Wait," I yelled back.

"Football is calling you, Kwaku. But Jesus is, too. How will you respond?"

"I . . . uh."

"You don't have to respond to me, Kwaku. Only to God. Talk to him. Admit you're a sinner. He will listen. You can ask him anything and tell him anything. But remember that he wants peace with you through Jesus Christ. Now go. Your friends are waiting."

"Thank you, Paul."

"No, Kwaku. Thank you for listening."

* * *

Unlike the previous week, I remembered everything he said. I began praying every night. I am sure my prayers sounded ineloquent, but they were sincere. I made my dreams my prayers. I prayed for freedom. To live in a big house with lots of money. To play football every day. To have anything I wanted. I thought that if I prayed hard enough, they would all come true. But I forgot about Jesus.

One night lying in bed, I whispered to John. "Do you know what kingdom work is?"

John opened his eyes and looked at me. "Kingdom what?"

"Kingdom work. That is what the man Paul has been talking to me about the last two Sundays. About peace with God. About Jesus."

"I know about Jesus, Kwaku. I am a Christian."

"What does it mean to be Christian?"

"It means you will live in Heaven."

I realised that I forgot what Paul said. I was asking for things I wanted, not what I needed. I needed salvation. That night, my prayers focused on my sin and Jesus saving me. I had peace with God. The first peace I had experienced in a long time.

NINE

I looked for Paul the next Sunday but could not find him. I wanted to tell him that I believed. That I had found peace with God. About my prayers.

We played football all day and finally stopped as the sun began to set. I walked towards our shanty with John, Lionel, and William.

"Hello, Kwaku." There stood Paul as we left the football pitch.

I waved. "Paul, you are here."

"Well, I have been here much of the day. I did not want to disturb your football match."

"You guys go ahead. I will be there soon," I said, waving away my fellow footballers.

"Paul, I have been praying. I was praying for things I wanted, but then I prayed about Jesus. To believe in Jesus for dying for my sins. Now I have peace with God. I am not mad anymore."

Paul's wide grin matched my own.

"I am delighted to hear that, Kwaku. I hoped you might say that. I also have something exciting to discuss with you. Come, let's walk."

We headed down the dirt trail. My stomach growled as we walked by a woman cooking banku. A slight breeze blew in from the lake. As much as I hated this place, it could be peaceful at times. This was one of those times.

I thought about this man next to me. Was he an angel? I had heard of angels, but was not sure what they looked like or what they did.

"On the way home last week, I told my daughter Bridget about our conversation. I gave her every detail about your life. She made a suggestion. At first, I dismissed her idea but then our family discussed it. My wife seemed accepting, but I was not so sure. Bridget became very persistent. She simply would not accept 'no' as an answer."

"What idea?"

"Kwaku, how would you feel about us adopting you?"

My eyes widened. "You mean come live with you?"

"Yes." He chuckled. "You will live with us. You will have a mother and father. You will have a sister and two brothers. You will be in our family."

My life as a slave made me suspicious, and I took one step back. "What do I have to do? What kind of work?"

"No work, Kwaku. You may have a few chores like the other children, but your work will be school."

"You will let me go to school?"

"Kwaku, there's a story in the Bible about a young man named Mephibosheth. He was the son of Jonathan and grandson of Saul. An orphan, just like you. King David adopted Mephibosheth. David told him that he would be just like his other sons and would always eat at his table." We stopped walking and Paul put his hand under my chin.

"Kwaku, you will be just like one of my sons. And you will always eat at my table."

"Like your sons?"

"Yes, Kwaku. My son."

My smile subsided thinking about how this would occur. "But I cannot simply run away. Master will beat me if I am caught."

Paul smiled. "No, Kwaku. You will not run away. We will talk with Master Ben and arrange for you to come."

"He will never let me go. He paid money for me. He is very particular."

"You let me worry about Master Ben. It might be better for now, if you do not discuss this with Master Ben. Do not lie. But do not offer the information. Master Ben has no legal right to keep you. I will work on this and be back in the next week or so."

Paul began to walk and turned back. "I'm glad you're agreeable. Had you said 'no,' I would be facing the wrath of Bridget." Paul laughed and walked away.

* * *

I desperately wanted to share my news with the others. That I might soon be free. Although Lionel had changed, I still did not trust him. I found my opportunity one day while we sat mending nets.

"Kwaku, what does that man keep talking to you about? The one on Sundays?" Lionel asked.

John and William looked up for my response.

I kept looking down at the net. "Nothing. Just about God and stuff like that."

Lionel scoffed. "What about God? You don't believe that stuff, do you, Kwaku?"

"Maybe. Maybe some of it. Maybe all of it. I like the man. I like what he says."

"I believe it all," John said. "I wish we could go to church. I miss things normal boys do like school, birthday parties . . . but I really miss church. I used to go all the time when I was younger. We sang, clapped, and danced. Our pastor taught us the Bible. It was fun."

Lionel objected again. "Kwaku. Don't be stupid. God does not—"

"Lionel, come here and help." Master Ben yelled from the shanty.

Lionel dropped his net and ran over.

I leaned in and whispered. "William, can you keep a secret?"

"Yes." William had become more and more talkative over the last year. He had matured from a scared five year-old boy to one that pulled in nets and worked harder than many boys older than him.

"William. That means you cannot tell anyone. Do you understand?" his brother John said.

Little William rolled his eyes. "Yes. I know. I understand."

I looked over both shoulders to make sure no one could hear. "I will go to church soon. And school. And birthday parties. And sleep in a bed. And eat good food every day."

"What are you talking about, Kwaku?" John said.

"The man that has been talking to me on Sundays. His name is Paul Boateng. He wants to adopt me." I checked Master Ben and Lionel again to make sure they could not hear. "Paul says I can come and live with him. He will work it out with Master Ben."

John leaned in. "Like that man that sold you to Master Ben?"

"Huh?" I said.

"How do you know this Paul is not another master? How do you know he is not buying you from Master Ben? Maybe he is tricking you like the man that brought you and Prince here. You must be careful, Kwaku."

I threw my net down. "Why are you saying that? You are just jealous."

"Shh. Kwaku. Not so loud. Listen. I want you to be adopted. I hope what this Mr Paul says is true. I am only saying to be careful."

I picked the net back up after calming down. "OK, but even if Paul makes me a slave, could it be any worse than this place?"

William remained silent and kept looking back and forth at our verbal sparring match.

John put his hand on my shoulder. "I want you to go, Kwaku. I hope he can convince Master Ben."

"OK, John. I am sorry. Paul is a very good talker. I think he will convince him."

* * *

I worried because Paul Boateng had not come in the last two weeks. Maybe he would never come back. Maybe he had changed his mind.

Lionel pulled our boat up to the shore to unload Monday morning's catch. An old red car was parked near the shanty. Master Ben walked around from the other side of the shanty to the lakeside arguing with someone. It was Paul. They seemed engaged in a heated discussion with lots of gesturing. John, William, and Ivy all watched from near the mango tree. Lionel and I ran up to hear.

"I'm telling you for the last time. No. You will not take him," Master Ben said, pointing a finger at Paul.

As we got closer, Lionel leaned towards me and whispered. "Who are they talking about? Who does this man want to take?"

"Me. That man wants to adopt me."

Lionel turned his head towards me—mouth opened wide. "That is the man you've been talking to on Sundays. Isn't it?"

"Yes."

John, William, and Ivy all knew, but I had managed to keep my secret from Lionel.

"You should hide, Kwaku. Master will be very mad at you," Lionel said.

Master Ben looked at me. "Kwaku, come here."

I walked slowly towards Master, keeping myself out of striking distance from his fist.

Master stepped towards me and put his hand under my chin, lifting it roughly. "Kwaku, what has this man told you? What lies has he put in your head?"

"He told me about having peace with God. About Jesus."

"Ha. Lies. All lies. There is no God. There is no Jesus. I am your Master. Do you understand?"

I do not know where it came from, but somewhere deep inside, I mustered up some courage. "No, you are not my master. There is a God. Jesus is my master now."

Ben turned towards Paul. "I will not stand for this. I will not let you fill this boy's head with lies."

Paul turned towards me. "It's time, Kwaku. We can go."

Ben stepped between us. "No. We will go to the village chief."

"I've already spoken to the chief of this village. I have shown him the paperwork from social welfare. He understands." Paul handed Ben several papers. "You see, Ben, I have been to Kumasi and retrieved his biological father's death certificate. I even found one for his mother in Accra. I have worked with the appropriate authorities and been granted custody of Kwaku. Shall we ask the Department of Social Welfare to come visit?"

Ben wagged his finger at Paul. "I paid for him. He is worth a lot of money. You would have to pay me a lot. He must work many more years for what I paid."

Paul shook his head left and right. "No, Ben. I will not give you any money."

Ben looked around. Everyone stared back in stunned silence. "What are you looking at? Get back to work. All of you." The others barely moved.

I stood still. Did that mean me as well?

"Kwaku! I said get to work."

I looked at Paul—my slave nature pulling me towards the lake and my free nature pulling towards Paul.

"No, Ben. Kwaku will work for you no longer. We are leaving." Paul motioned for me to come. "Let's go, Kwaku."

Ben stood by the old upside down boat near the shanty. The one he bent me over to whip me with his cane. He picked up the old paddle that lay near. The one he used to kill Prince. The scene of my worst moment as a slave. A slave master with an old paddle separated me from Paul and freedom. I thought of Prince's bravery. He would have gone through Ben. He would have fought his way.

I looked at Ivy. No noise came from her mouth, but she mouthed the word go.

John smiled at me and nodded.

I made one step towards Paul. Ben lifted the paddle.

"Ben," Paul said.

Ben ignored him. I thought Paul might fight him for me.

He said it louder. "Ben!"

This time Ben—with rage in his eyes—turned towards him. "What!"

"Ben, it's time to put the paddle down." Paul stood, expressionless, with his hands behind his back. He had lowered his voice to a normal level. "Ben, I serve the God Most High. This is his will. I will take care of this boy now. God has granted his care and upbringing to me."

Ben did not look back at me. He dropped the paddle and walked into the shanty.

Ivy, John, and little William ran up and hugged me. Lionel just looked—expressionless.

I hopped in the front seat of the car with a huge smile.

Paul sat down and started the car.

"I am surprised the village chief let me go. He and Ben are friends. They drink together."

Paul smiled. "Well, Kwaku, I would not say he let you go. I only told Ben that I showed the chief the paperwork and that he understands. The chief said he would not help me, and that I should forget the matter because Ben will not comply. I politely told him 'thank you' and walked away. I prayed that Ben would not seek out the chief. I prayed that Ben would not be violent. I prayed that God would bless our efforts."

"God answered your prayers," I said.

He turned towards me. "Yes, he has. Let's go home, Kwaku."

I wore only a shirt and shorts. I had no other belongings, sandals, suitcase, or keepsakes. But I had one other thing. Something of great value. Something Prince died trying to achieve. I had Freedom.

TEN

"Almost home, Kwaku. Do you remember much about Accra?"

"Not really. Just the guest home and Agbogbloshie. My sister may still be there. Can we go find her?"

"Of course, Kwaku. My wife Thelma and I have already discussed this. We knew that adopting you meant trying to find your sister and adopting her as well."

"You will adopt her?" I sat forward in my seat. "How far is Agbogbloshie?"

Paul laughed. "We will go soon. Let's get you home, bathed, and in some new clothes. I am sure Ma is cooking dinner as we speak. I'll bet you'd love a nice meal?"

My mouth watered at the thought.

"We will go tomorrow after a good rest. You've had a very eventful day already."

Several tall buildings shot up over the horizon as we approached Accra.

"Kwaku, it occurs to me that I said, 'Ma is cooking dinner.' Our children call us Daa and Ma. But we understand you may not be ready for that. We know you still have many thoughts about your father and mummy and miss them very much."

"I want to call you Daa and Ma. I want to badly."

"Then, so be it." Daa used an official sounding voice. "Henceforth, from this day forward, Stephen "Kwaku" Ghansah shall refer to Paul and Thelma Boateng as Daa and Ma."

We both laughed.

After the laughing died down a bit, I thought about my last name, Ghansah. The name of my biological father. The name of my biological family and heritage.

"Daa, do I have to change my name to Boateng?"

"Kwaku, you are my son now. But that right and privilege comes from God's will, not an earthly name. You may choose. If you want to keep your biological father's name, I will take no offence."

"I think I will remain a Ghansah out of respect for him."

"I'm very proud of you, Kwaku. That is indeed a respectable thing to do."

The car slowed as we entered the traffic of Accra. My last trip to Accra had been on a hot and crowded bus with my mum and sister—all of us heartbroken over losing Father. This time, joy filled my heart at the endless possibilities. My new family and school. I could not wait to attend school.

As we came to stop at a traffic light, a man waved belts at me hoping to make a sale. Soon, twenty others had walked by with various goods. One woman's head tray seemed to reach higher than the *trotro* next to us. Other people walked up and down the street, most in a particular state of hurry.

Several boys ran down a street in their school uniforms—bright blue shorts with crisp checked shirts. Sleek and smart. I envied them. I wondered if my uniform would look like that. We happened to head down that road and on the right emerged a football pitch with green grass. There was not a spot of dirt. Players ran up and down the field in bright uniforms and shiny boots. We stopped at another light and I rolled down my window. I had hoped the light lasted a long time so I could watch.

I stuck my head out of the window and took in a big whiff of air.

"Kwaku, what do you smell. Smog from the cars?"

"No, Daa. It is what I do not smell. I do not smell the lake."

After passing a large church, we turned onto a dirt road. Daa drove slowly as the car rode up and down with every dip and bump.

"Well, Kwaku, this is home."

A tall beige wall topped with barbed wire surrounded the house with only its red roof visible. The green gate with gold ornate spikes seemed magical to me. A gate to a new life, freedom, and possibilities.

Daa honked the horn. Bridget—my new sister—poked her head out. She looked at me, smiling, and opened the gate. We drove in to see a large sign that said, WELCOME HOME KWAKU.

"That is for me," I said, stating the obvious.

"Yes, Kwaku. You are home now."

I exited the car slowly. Bridget greeted me first.

"Welcome, Kwaku. Do you remember me?"

I nodded.

"I am Thelma. You are most welcome," Ma said, offering me a hug.

Daa corrected her. "No, Ma. You are Ma and I am Daa. It's been officially decreed."

"Well, OK, Kwaku. I am Ma."

"Hello, Ma," I said.

Her eyes began to water.

Two boys stood next to one another but neither moved.

"Come, boys," Daa said, waving them over. "Kwaku, meet your brothers. This is Thomas and Derek."

Thomas, 14 years old, smiled and held out his hand. "You are welcome, Kwaku."

An older brother. I always wanted an older brother. A great protector—like Mercy. Someone to look up to—figuratively and literally, as he stood one foot taller than me.

Derek held out his hand but offered no smile. "Hello."

I immediately sensed his ambivalence towards me. He looked away the moment we shook hands. We looked nothing alike, but shared the same height, build, and age.

"Kwaku, Derek and you are the same age," Ma said. "12."

"I am 12?"

Derek scoffed. "You don't know how old you are?"

"Uh…yes, I am 12."

I actually did not know. I lost track of time and dates as a slave. I was 11 years old when Simon sold me to Ben, but my birthday came and went without me knowing it.

I could just as easily have been 13 by now. Slaves do not celebrate birthdays or use calendars. Slave time is lost time.

Ma put her arm around me. "I'll bet you are very hungry. Do you like khebabs?"

"Oh yes, Ma! I have not eaten khebabs in so long."

The smell of khebabs greeted me at the threshold.

"Come, Kwaku. Let me show you where you will sleep," Thomas said. Derek did not join us.

The home appeared small from the front, but once inside, hallways connected several rooms. We meandered towards the back of the house and entered our bedroom.

Thomas held up his hands with palms up. "Well, what do you think?"

"It is very nice." The room was twice the size of the room five of us shared in Ben's shanty.

"That's my bed," Thomas said, pointing to a single bed on one side of the room. He pointed to bunk beds on the other side. "That is yours."

I walked over and ran my hand across the top bunk feeling the white sheets.

"No! That is my bed. Yours is the bottom." We both turned to find Derek standing in the doorway. "I sleep on the top one." He walked over and stood next to the bunk beds as if guarding them.

"Calm yourself, Derek," Thomas said.

I hardly knew Derek, but he reminded me a lot of Lionel.

"I do not mind the bottom bed. That will be fine," I said.

Bridget appeared in the doorway. "Time to eat. I hope you are hungry, Kwaku." She lifted her heels and walked away—a vivacious girl. I noticed she almost jumped in the air every time she moved. Energetic. Full of life. I loved her immediately.

Derek walked by me and out of the room. Thomas put his arm around me, leading me to dinner. "Don't worry about Derek. He can be stubborn."

I had not sat at a table for a meal in over a year. As slaves, we ate all our meals under the huge mango tree or next to the shanty.

"I know you must be very hungry, Kwaku. We will fill your belly and then you can bathe," Ma said.

A white tablecloth covered the large table. Ma and Bridget placed items on the table as they sat. Ma served my food. I sank my teeth into the kebab.

"Kwaku, I know you are hungry. But we must first offer thanks," Daa said.

I looked left and right with everyone staring at me and deduced he meant prayer.

Daa smiled. "Bow your heads. Most Heavenly Father, we are thankful for providing food for our family once again. We are thankful for your daily provision. And we are especially thankful for bringing Kwaku into our home. Amen."

I looked left and right, unsure if I could eat now.

Bridget, sitting next to me, leaned over and whispered. "OK, now you can eat."

I loved the khebab. I hardly tasted it eating so fast. I finally slowed down and enjoyed every bit of this delicacy.

* * *

I had not taken a bath since we stayed in the guest home over one year ago. Not a real bath. Sometimes we would bathe in the lake and might even share a bar of soap. But we emerged from the water smelling like the lake. Hardly a clean feeling. The warm bathwater running over my fingers spread a feeling of warmth throughout my body. My tired bones ached far more than they should for a boy my age. I felt like an overworked old man.

My bare feet cooled on the linoleum floor. The whole bathroom looked clean. The only thing out of place was me. I slid off my filthy clothes, wondering if they should be burned.

Thomas walked in with some clothes and gasped. "What happened to your backside? What are those marks?"

I looked over my shoulder and rubbed the raised marks. I had never actually seen them, but then looked in the mirror. "That is where Master Ben caned me."

"I'm so sorry, Kwaku. These are some clean clothes for you," Thomas said, backing out of the bathroom still looking at the cane marks.

I looked at myself for a long time in the mirror. Staring at the former slave. I liked the way freedom looked.

I stepped into the tub and eased down in the water. A full belly and warm water. And a little later, clean sheets. I hadn't been this relaxed in a long time.

Knock! Knock!

"Kwaku, are you almost finished? We are about to start our family devotion time," Bridget said.

"Uh…yes. I'll be right out."

I had no idea what family devotion time meant, but assumed I needed to attend. I drained the tub, leaving behind a year's worth of dirt and grime and slipped on the clean clothes.

I walked into the living room but saw no one.

Bridget waved from the back porch. "We're out here, Kwaku."

The whole family sat down, Bibles in laps. I chose an empty chair. Only two of the eight chairs on the porch matched.

Derek sat up and leaned forward. "Hey, why is he wearing my clothes? I did not give them to him."

"You mean those pants you haven't worn in over a month?" Ma said. "You mean that shirt that has hung in the back of your closet that you've never worn? Derek, whose clothes are they?"

Derek lowered his head. "God's."

"That's right," Ma said. "He owns the cattle on a thousand hills. Everything you see, including the clothes on our backs belong to God. We're mere stewards of them for a time." Ma lifted her Bible. "Just like this Bible that I have been a steward of for a long time. Kwaku, this is now your Bible to steward. The most important thing you need to know about the Bible is to read it daily and do what it says."

"Thank you."

The Bible's binding barely contained the pages within. Several almost fell out. I thumbed through it, noticing marks and words written in the margins on nearly every page. Hardly the kind of gift you would unwrap, but at least I had my own Bible.

After prayers, Bridget read the first chapter of Joshua. I followed along the best I could but had trouble understanding some of the strange words like Euphrates and Hittites.

Daa took off his glasses. "Ma already stated one of the themes of this chapter . . . to read the Bible daily and follow its instructions. What would you say is another one of the themes of this chapter?"

"For Joshua to be strong and courageous," Thomas said.

"That's right," Daa said. "Only be strong and courageous."

I laid my head on the pillow that night thinking about those words. Strong and courageous. Could I be strong and courageous? Always? I had to be. I had to be so we could find Mercy.

ELEVEN

As promised, Daa started the car for our seek-and-find mission to Agbogbloshie.

"I know finding Mercy is very important to you, Kwaku. I found someone who may be able to help. He's an evangelist named Kofi that used to live there. He visits there often."

We stopped at a church and a man looking no older than 18 got in the front seat.

He turned and looked over his left shoulder. "You must be Kwaku. I am Kofi. Paul here has told me your story. I'm sorry for the way you were treated. That people take advantage like that." He shook his head. "But you have found favour with God. The Boatengs are a fine family."

I leaned up in my seat. "Do you know a man named Simon?"

"Yes, I've heard of him. He's very dangerous. I've heard of him tricking boys and taking them to Lake Volta."

"Yes, that is what he did to me."

"Unfortunately, there are many like him. I heard the police arrested him for some other crimes and sent him to prison."

"What about Auntie Agnes? Have you heard of her?" I asked.

Kofi shook his head. "Sorry, I have not. We will ask around though. Hopefully, we can find your sister. Surely, someone knows her. It may not be easy. Thousands live there."

I wished I had remembered the location of her shanty. But the maze of structures all looked the same to me.

We stopped at a traffic light on the outskirts of Agbogbloshie. I noticed two soldiers in crisp uniforms walking tall. I instantly thought of Prince. I thought of his bravery. He would have made a fine soldier.

Kofi looked at Daa and then me. "Listen, we must be careful as we move around. There are good places here but also bad places with robbers. Agbogbloshie is my home. Just follow me."

We stopped the car several times with Kofi asking if anyone knew Auntie Agnes. This went on for hours. Nearly every time Kofi rolled down his window, the smell of Agbogbloshie entered the car. Not every part of Agbogbloshie smelled bad and some parts were nice. Not this part though.

Flies attacked our car from every angle. I swatted them away with little success. I do not know how Kofi could hear with so many people shouting while selling their goods. The activity made the place seem chaotic.

"Maybe we should stop for the day," Daa said.

"No, we cannot. We must keep trying. Please," I said.

"OK, maybe a little longer."

I grabbed Kofi's shoulder. "Maybe we should ask a *kayayoo*"

Kofi and Daa looked at each other.

"We've only been asking adults. The *kayayei* know many people like Auntie Agnes. Great idea, Kwaku," Kofi said.

We parked the car and all three of us began asking every *kayayoo* we could find. We came back together on the corner of two roads with no success.

A *kaya* started pushing his cart and then stopped and turned around. "Oh, wait. Auntie Agnes. A big woman that laughs a lot. She starts and ends many of her sentences with a 'heh, heh.'"

I darted towards him. "That is her."

"I believe her shanty is on the other side of the dump." He proceeded to give Kofi more detailed directions.

We hopped in the car and headed straight there. I knew we were closer to finding Mercy. The directions from the *kaya* were not exactly detailed. Kofi had to ask at least three others for landmarks, but after about 45 minutes, a young woman pointed us towards Auntie Agnes' shanty. As soon as the car turned that direction, I remembered the area.

Kofi turned towards me. "Does this look familiar?"

"Yes. Yes, I know this. Keep driving straight. Her shanty is on the right."

We inched closer. Several pedestrians and *kayayei* blocked us from moving forward. Finally, we reached it.

"That is it." I jumped out of the car.

"Kwaku, stop. Wait for us. You must let us talk," Daa said.

As we walked up to the shanty, Auntie Agnes walked out.

I pulled at her arm. "Auntie Agnes! Auntie Agnes! Do you remember me? Kwaku."

"Heh, heh. Who, boy? Who are you?"

"I am Kwaku. I was your *kaya*. My sister Mercy—"

Daa put his hand over my mouth. "Excuse me, ma'am. My name is Paul. This is my son, Kwaku, and our friend, Kofi. About one year ago, Kwaku here and another boy, Prince, worked for you as *kaya*."

She tilted her head back. "Ah, yes. You boys ran off and left my carts. Cost me a lot of money. Why did you run off, boy?"

"I—" I began to speak but Daa again placed his hand over my mouth.

Kofi leaned in. "Ma'am. I'm afraid these boys were deceived and taken by a man named Simon and sold for fishing on Lake Volta."

"Heh, heh. Well, I told these boys to be careful. I know that Simon. 'He's a bad man.'"

"We are looking for Kwaku's sister, Mercy," Kofi said. "Is she here?"

"No, she's not here. She ran off several months ago. She was trouble and always complaining about her work, heh, heh." She turned away from us and started to sweep in front of her shanty.

"Maybe it was the kind of work you made her do," I said.

Auntie Agnes turned and stared at me—brows furrowed.

Daa gently grabbed my shoulders. "Kwaku, please. You must let us handle this. It is a delicate situation. Can you remain quiet while we do that?"

"Yes, sir. I am sorry."

"It's OK."

Auntie Agnes began to walk away.

Kofi ran over and stopped her. "Please, do you know where she went?"

"No, I don't know. These kids. They come, and they go. She is probably working for someone else."

"What about Prince's family? Where are they? What was his last name?" Daa said.

"I don't know. Prince showed up one day looking for work so I hired him. I don't know where his family is."

I had hoped we could find Prince's family and tell them what happened to him. I never learned his last name, and he likely never knew mine. Slaves do not need last names. I doubted we would ever be able to find anyone who knew Prince. Daa thought it unlikely that the police would do much about Ben killing Prince. Slave masters get away with things like that. While finding Mercy remained my priority, I desired some justice for Prince or at least some closure for his family.

Kofi continued pressing Auntie Agnes about both Prince and Mercy but nothing came of it.

We got back into the car.

"What now?" I said.

Kofi looked at me and then back at Daa. "I know of another place here at Agbogbloshie, where many girls . . . uh . . . work."

"It's OK, Kofi," Daa said. "Kwaku knows the kind of work his sister was forced to do."

We entered a part of Agbogbloshie I had not seen before. Although it resembled other parts of this area with small shops and *kayayei*, it seemed even more crowded. I could hardly see through the mass of people walking or standing around. People on foot zipped by us as we stood still in the traffic. No bad smell there.

I noticed one woman stumbling as she walked and another trying to hold her up. She appeared drunk. She stepped off into the open sewer and sat there in defeat. Her companion yelled at her and walked away. I am sure Daa preferred I had not seen these things, but I had seen many drunken people in the fishing village.

"We must stay in the car," Kofi said. "This is a dangerous area."

As the car inched forward in the congested traffic, I noticed several women standing together. I looked away then turned back quickly. I saw Mercy talking with two other women. At the same instant, the traffic opened up and Daa sped away. The women started walking off in the other direction.

"Mercy!"

I leaned forward and slapped the headrest behind Daa. "Stop the car! Stop the car! I saw Mercy!"

Daa slammed on the brakes.

Kofi looked over. "Where? Are you sure?"

"Yes. She is wearing a yellow dress. We must go. They are walking away."

"Let me park, Kwaku," Daa said.

Cars soon clustered all around us and traffic jammed. We could not move in any direction.

"Hurry, Daa. We will lose them."

Mercy and the group of women continued walking farther away from us.

"Hold on, Kwaku. I'm trying to move."

The women turned a corner around a building. I knew we would lose them. I jumped out of the car into the middle of the street.

"Kwaku, no!" Daa said.

A truck slammed on its brakes before it could hit me. The driver honked and yelled, but I could not hear what were likely curses. A motorcycle riding between the lanes whizzed by me. I manoeuvred my way through traffic and ran towards Mercy. I noticed Kofi had got out of the car and ran a few steps behind me.

We reached the corner of the building where I last saw them. I looked right and left but did not see them. Then I heard giggling. They had crossed the street and headed towards an alley.

"Mercy! Mercy!"

Why did she not hear me?

Kofi put his arm against my chest. "Wait for the traffic to pass."

"Mercy! Stop!" I yelled.

A few people stared at my continued yelling.

"OK, let's go." I lifted up Kofi's arm and ran across the street.

"Mercy!"

They turned another corner, but we gained distance on them. I turned the same corner and there they stood. All three of them. Mercy had her back to me. I grabbed her arm and turned her.

"Mercy!"

The woman looked at me.

"Mercy?" I said. "Are you Mercy?"

"No," she said coldly, and turned back towards her friends.

She looked like Mercy. But I knew it was not her as soon as I saw her face up close. Head hung low, I walked away.

"Excuse me," Kofi said. "Do any of you know a woman named Mercy?" I turned to hear their response but had no hope that they knew her.

They simply shook their heads.

Kofi put his hand on my back and we returned to the car. Daa had parked and stood by the car waiting. He had many reasons to be upset with me. I walked up to him—head down and drooped shoulders.

"Let's go home, Kwaku. We will try again, soon. We will keep trying."

* * *

I plodded in the front door to see Ma greeting me.

"Kwaku, how—"

I walked right past her and headed straight for my room.

Ma walked in a few minutes later. "Daa has told me what happened. I am so sorry, Kwaku."

I sat on the bed staring at the floor. "It is like I lost her again."

"I know, Kwaku. You must have faith that this is God's plan. You must pray. Pray that God will reunite you with Mercy one day. Pray often."

I noticed she held something behind her back.

"You must sleep well tonight," she said. "Tomorrow you start school."

Thinking of school made me feel much better. So many of my dreams had come true. First, a family and now school.

"You know, Kwaku, you must have a uniform for school."

She pulled the clothes from behind her back. The dark brown shorts had creases down the front. The collared shirt had a green-checked pattern with a patch on the pocket.

I read the words on the patch. Ut Omnes Unum Sint. "What kind of words are those?"

Ma smiled. "It's Latin. That all may be one. It means that even though we may look different, have different backgrounds, or have different talents, we can work together for the good of all. Notice the logo looks like piano keys. You can play just the white keys and make music and you can play just the black keys and make music, but if you play them both, you have harmony."

I nodded, agreeably.

"Jesus desires for us to have that kind of unity. It is a good thing."

I frowned. "I do not think I will help anyone. I have not been to school in a year. They will think I am stupid. What if the teacher asks me something and I do not know the answer?"

"Kwaku. You are not stupid. You are one of the smartest and bravest boys I know. I only recently met you but can tell already. You will do great things at Achimota School. You will do great things for God. You must have Colossians 3:23 as your motto. Whatever you do, do your work heartily, as for the Lord rather than men. Do your school for God, Kwaku. Do it all for him. And leave the results up to him.

"Why don't you try on the uniform?" She laid the clothes on my bed and walked out.

I put them on and looked at myself in the mirror, amazed at the transformation. I felt a sense of dignity. Belonging. A bit of confidence even crept in.

TWELVE

"Kwaku, let me tell you about the value of education," Daa said.

Thomas looked over from the front seat of the car to Derek and smiled as we pulled out of the gate for the ride to school.

"Here comes the big speech, Kwaku," Derek said.

Daa smiled as well. "Thomas and Derek are poking fun at me because they've heard this speech many times. But it still rings true and will likely ring true for many years to come. You see, I grew up poor."

"So did we," Thomas said. He and Derek laughed.

Daa got serious—brows furrowed. "I wouldn't exactly call us poor. We are far from wealthy, but none of you are wanting for food, clothing, or shelter, are you?"

They did not respond.

"As I was saying, my father managed to put me through school. I loved it and studied very hard. My father would say, 'Education is the key to prosperity.'"

I noticed Derek mouthing the quote.

Daa held up his index finger to make his point. "You must remember that, Kwaku. Your mind is powerful. You must learn to use it wisely. By studying hard and improving your mind, you will reap great benefits for yourself, your family, and most importantly, for God's Kingdom. What is your favourite subject, Kwaku?"

I looked out the window pondering the question. "I do not know. Maybe reading. I love to read."

"Me too, Kwaku," Thomas said. "I read all the time. I want to study literature in the university."

Daa held up his finger again. "Kwaku, you should always have a book. Always be reading in your spare time. Fill your mind with history, adventure, and philosophy. Read poetry. Read, read, read," he said, wagging his finger each time for emphasis.

"Do you like to read, Derek?" I asked.

Derek merely shrugged his shoulders. He had maintained his animosity towards me from the moment we met. I resolved to make him like me.

We came out of a traffic circle and turned down a road with trees hovering on both sides.

"This is it," Thomas said.

We drove between two large white pillars. The school campus lay between a forest reserve and busy Accra streets. Several white buildings connected the open layout.

Thomas and Derek darted off after we parked the car. I noticed that Derek had joined a group of several boys— all smiling and laughing. I hoped they would accept me in the same manner. I longed for that kind of sincere camaraderie. John and Ivy were friends, but we had few joyful moments. I yearned for a group of friends with whom to share my life.

We entered one of the many large buildings. It all seemed so official. Shiny floors and high ceilings. We sat outside the office of the headmaster, Mr Quaye.

A woman walked out of the office and cleared her throat. "Headmaster Quaye will see you shortly, Mr Boateng."

"You know, Kwaku, I sat in these very chairs with my father many years ago waiting to see the headmaster."

"You went to school here?"

"I did. Many years ago. Unfortunately, I didn't want to be here at first. I told you I loved school, but in the beginning, I rebelled. I found no reason to study mathematics and science. It seemed useless. The truth is, I was lazy and did not want to do the work. After a few days of this, my father told me a story."

Daa cleared his throat. "A wise old man took his grandson for a walk. He told him to pull a weed from the ground—roots and all. The boy pulled it from the ground, effortlessly. He told him to remember how easy it was. They continued their walk. He told him to pull up a much larger weed that was as tall as his waist. The boy pulled very hard and finally it came up, roots and all. After a few minutes, the grandfather pointed to a small tree. The boy pulled and pulled but never managed to pull it out of the ground. The grandfather looked at his grandson and said, 'What seems easy now will become much harder later in life.'"

I stared at Daa with a blank face.

"You see, Kwaku, as a boy, I may have been able to do easy things like pulling up that small weed, but one day, I'd need all that math and science and other school subjects to tackle that tree that will most certainly need to be uprooted."

Daa put his hand on my shoulder. "Just because I did not understand why my teachers taught me certain things, I had to be confident that it was in my best interest to learn and excel in my studies. Do you understand?"

"Paul." The headmaster walked out of his office and greeted us before I could respond. "And you must be Kwaku."

"Yes, sir."

"Please, come in."

Headmaster Quaye's office smelled like old books. Hundreds of them lined the walls all around us. We sat across from his desk which had several stacks of papers on top. All of them neatly placed. There seemed no disorder about him or his office.

"Please, Kwaku, this is Headmaster Quaye."

Mr Quaye nodded and Daa turned to me.

"Mr Quaye, this is Stephen Ghansah. He goes by Kwaku.

I had never experienced the formal Ghanaian greeting where I was one of the main participants.

Mr Quaye cleared his throat. "You are welcome. What do you think of the school so far, Kwaku?"

I looked out the window and noticed several boys and girls walking in different directions.

I looked back at Mr Quaye. "It is busy."

He laughed. "Yes, it is busy. We want to be busy about education. Our mission is to build men and women of integrity. We build future leaders. We want..."

The headmaster went on for several minutes about the motto and other things with Daa nodding, approvingly. I tuned him out once I noticed a boy outside the window dribbling a football as he went along the path—juggling books in his arms. That is what I wanted to do. Sure, I wanted to go to class and learn, but I wanted to play football. Dreams of making tremendous goals for the Ghana Black Stars could always provide me an escape.

The meeting ended with Daa leaving and the headmaster escorting me to class. I had felt some jitters as we drove up, but now felt more confident. It was a school. Everything would be fine.

* * *

I made my way from one class to the next. The teachers did their best to ease me into school life and made no great demands of me. I collected one textbook after another.

Lunch presented my first opportunity to meet some of the other students. A sea of people surrounded me in the enormous dining hall. I noticed Derek pretending not to see me and found an empty seat. I held my head up and pretended to enjoy my food but felt very lonely.

"How are your classes?"

I looked up to see Thomas.

"OK."

He sat down, and a few of his friends joined us. "How was your meeting with the headmaster?"

"Uh . . . good, I guess."

Thomas elbowed his friend and smiled. "Did he tell you about the future leaders we will be?"

I smiled back. "Yes. How did you know he—"

"He gives that speech to everyone." He stood up. "We must go. See you later, Kwaku."

"Bye."

He stopped and looked back. "Oh, do you have Mrs Mantey for social studies?"

I glanced at my schedule. "Yes."

He and his friends laughed. "Good luck."

I finished my lunch and left the building for my next class pondering Thomas' comment.

I poked my head into Mrs Mantey's classroom with caution. Thomas' insincere "good luck" concerned me.

Was this woman mean? Demanding? Does she hate new students?

I made my way in and approached the lady at the desk, handing her my schedule.

"Madam, I am a new student."

She kept her head down perusing a book. "One moment."

I looked around and noticed the other students staring back. Some smiled and some snickered. The blackboard looked as if it had experienced heavy use with more white spaces from erasures than fresh green spots. Unlike the headmaster, papers littered her desk—strewn about in no sensible order.

She noticed the snickering and looked up. "Quiet."

She looked at me, her head slightly tilted down so her eyes could look over the glasses that rested on the end of her nose. "And who do we have here?"

"I am Kwaku, Madam."

"Well . . . Kwaku. You are welcome. Have a seat over there." She pointed to an empty seat in the front row.

A girl next to me—wearing glasses—smiled, offering some comfort. "Hello. I'm Georgina."

I waved back, failing to offer an audible response.

Mrs Mantey stood up, pushed her glasses up her nose, and grabbed a piece of chalk. "We've been discussing Kwame Nkrumah's relationship with the British. I want us to consider some of his quotes. Let's try to understand his reason for saying them and their impact." She looked down at a book on her desk. "He said, 'We face neither East nor West; we face forward.' Why did he say that?"

She looked up and spanned the class. I did the same and saw no raised hands.

"Kwaku. I know you are new, but why don't you try to answer? What did Kwame Nkrumah mean by, 'We face neither East nor West; we face forward'?"

"Who, Madam?"

A loud burst of laughter broke out.

Mrs Mantey looked away from me. "Silence!"

She turned back. "Kwame Nkrumah, the first president of Ghana." She paused, staring at me. "Kwaku, you will learn much in this classroom. Georgina, you answer."

Geogina sat up in her seat and leaned forward, lecturing with her hand. "We control our destiny rather than the West, for example, and we should…"

Geogina's answer seemed brilliant. I sank in my seat, mortified. How could I have forgotten who the first president of Ghana was? I knew about him. I had studied about him in school. My brain went blank. Too nervous.

Class ended, and I tried to sneak by Mrs Mantey.

Without looking up, she said, "Kwaku, why don't you see me after your final class." She looked up, eyebrows raised. "Understand?"

"Yes, madam."

Already in trouble. On the first day of school. What would Daa say? Would he be disappointed? Would he regret adopting me?

* * *

My final class ended. I found Thomas and told him to tell Daa my fate so he would not worry.

He laughed. "Don't worry, Kwaku. Mrs Mantey will not bite you. Just a thorough scolding."

I entered Mrs Mantey's classroom much the same as earlier—by poking my head in the door.

"Kwaku, come here and let me show you something."

She opened a book to a marked page. "How is your reading?"

"Good, Madam. I read very well."

"Excellent. Read this part here aloud. The part that is marked."

I bent over for a closer look. "Freedom is not something that one people can bestow on another as a gift. They claim it as their own and none can keep it from them."

"President Nkrumah said that. The same man who said the quote I asked you about in class. I would venture to guess this is a quote you understand better than anyone in all my classes and perhaps anyone in this school. The headmaster told me of your background. I should never have called on you like that during the lecture. I am sorry."

I stood up straight and smiled not knowing what to say.

"I want you to walk somewhere with me."

We left the large white building and walked towards another.

"President Nkrumah went to school here. He walked these very grounds. He probably sat in a classroom and did not know the answer to a question his teacher asked." She smiled. "Don't let the incident today bother you. You may have some catching-up to do as far as your studies, but I will bet you can do it."

We entered a room with books as far as I could see. I noticed a peculiar dusty smell. Several students busied themselves looking over the rows of books. One student sat at a desk with at least five books opened to various pages. An older lady pushed a cart full of books.

Mrs Mantey spread out her hands. "This is our library, Kwaku. This is where you can catch up. I don't mean that you need to study in this room, but these books are the tools you will use to reach your true potential. My fellow teachers and I will certainly require much of you, and I would like you to always have a book from this library with you wherever you go."

I followed her through the rows of bookcases as she continued her speech. "I don't mean you cannot spend time with friends and play football, but think of all the time you will have to read. While you are waiting for the *trotro*, when the rain comes and you cannot go outside, and before you go to sleep at night. Think of the opportunities."

Rest assured, her little talk did not fall on deaf ears. I walked around and imagined all that I could learn. Slavery had deprived me of the joy of books.

She reached towards a shelf and handed me a book.

I read the title, *Ghana: The Autobiography of Kwame Nkrumah*. Flipping through the pages, I noticed its wear. Many students must have read this book.

"Why don't you try this one first? There may be some politics you wouldn't understand, but read about the man."

The librarian instructed me regarding the proper procedures for borrowing a book from the library; a task I would perform many times.

I met Daa in the car at the agreed pick-up spot. Thomas and Derek sat in the car reading, while Daa read a newspaper.

"What did Mrs Mantey want?" Thomas asked.

During the ride home, I shared about my entire day. I had experienced a flood of emotions. The other students laughing at me was certainly a low point, but the library made up for that. My future seemed bright. My constant dreams while fishing on the lake were all coming true. Dreams of a family, siblings, and school.

I laid in bed that night holding the book from the library. A little lamp attached to the headboard illuminated the cover. *Ghana: The Autobiography of Kwame Nkrumah*. Nkrumah. A great name. I wanted to learn more about his life, education, struggles, and the Gold Coast. I was ready to learn.

THIRTEEN

The first two days of school went well as Sunday approached, and with it the opportunity for me to experience another first—church. Sure, I had been to church in the past, attended school, and taken hot baths before I became an orphan, but my new life allowed me to enjoy these firsts again.

The church building drew people in by car, *trotro*, taxi, and on foot. We walked since we lived less than a mile away. I wore slacks and a pressed white shirt—more clothes borrowed from Derek's wardrobe, angering him. I clutched my Bible, ready to use it at a moment's notice.

"Please, this is our son, Kwaku," Daa said, introducing me to one of many that day.

Ma, Bridget, and Thomas did the same with their friends. I must have met fifty people at church, instantly forgetting their names.

We sat in a long pew and our family nearly filled it. The worship music vibrated throughout the building and I clapped and sang along. I loved the joyful noise and unity.

The pastor spoke for a long time, and I must confess I understood little of it.

"But Jacob said, 'Swear to me first.' So he swore an oath to him, selling his birthright to Jacob," the pastor read, from the book of Genesis.

That part I understood. I could not believe someone would give away their birthright—their place in the family—for stew.

We prayed and sang more. Congregants clutched money in their hands and placed it in the offering basket. We had many more greetings.

I remembered John telling me how much he missed church. He would say things like, "I want to be free to worship."

That is what freedom gave me. The ability to worship with my family. And I loved it.

We left church but Daa led us a different way than the way home.

"Where are we going?" I asked.

Ma smiled and put her arm around me. "We have a surprise for you, Kwaku."

I stepped ahead of everyone and turned around walking backwards. "What? What surprise?"

"You will see," she said.

We arrived at a hotel restaurant a few blocks from the church. Another first for me. Another new thing with my new family.

Bridget put her arm around my elbow. "We never get to eat in restaurants. This is a real treat."

I noticed she had been carrying a bag all morning but never asked what it contained.

The menu offered so many choices. Traditional Ghanaian dishes but also many Western dishes.

"I think I'll have the *kelewele* to begin, followed by soup, and Tilapia with banku for my main course," Thomas announced.

Daa looked at him sternly. "No, you will not. You may order one regular-sized dish. Do you think we are wealthy?"

"I'm having the jollof rice," Bridget said.

Thomas laid down his menu in mock frustration. "But I thought we were celebrating Kwaku's—" Thomas covered his mouth with his hand.

Everyone looked at Thomas.

His eyes widened and he moved back in his seat. "Oops."

Ma patted his wrist. "That's OK, Thomas. We can make our announcement now." She turned to me. "We have a surprise for you, Kwaku. Do you know what today is?"

"Sunday," I said.

"Yes, it is Sunday. But do you know what day of the year?"

I looked off to the side in thought.

Ma clapped her hands. "It's your birthday. Happy birthday! You are 13 years old today."

"Happy birthday," said the others. Derek even managed a mumbled version.

"While I was working with social welfare for your adoption, they did some background investigations and found a record of your birth in Kumasi. You were born this day, 13 years ago. So, happy birthday!" Daa said.

I sat there, mouth wide open. "Today is my birthday," awkwardly repeating the obvious.

Bridget reached down for the mysterious bag she had been carrying. "Here is your present, Kwaku."

She pulled a funny-shaped box from the plain brown paper bag. Red wrapping with various gold cubicle designs covered the object that was rounded on two sides with sharp edges over the centre. I started to peel away but decided on a more efficient method and ripped the paper off.

"A football!" My mouth agape signalled both my surprise and pleasure. "My own football!"

I removed the square cardboard covering the ball and spun it in my hands. It had the traditional design with a white base and red pentagons.

"Thank you. Thank you so much."

"You're welcome. We're glad you like it."

* * *

Like the boy I saw outside the headmaster's window the week before, I walked to class Monday morning dribbling my football. Everyone else moved with a purpose. I had no purpose—at least not yet—other than to go to class.

Achimota school offered so many opportunities. I read most of the weekend and finished President Nkrumah's autobiography. Much of the politics confused me, but I certainly admired the man and learned much about the history of Ghana. I planned to visit the library and check out another book. Having toured most of the buildings at the school, I saw endless activities I might try. Art, music, drama, and sports such as basketball, cricket, squash, swimming, and of course, football.

Thump!

My ball. Someone came from the side and kicked my ball.

"Ato, pass me the ball," Edward said with a raised hand.

I knew Derek's friends, Ato and Edward. I saw the three of them together many times and Thomas had told me their names. I had hoped Derek would invite me to join their group at lunch, but he never did.

They passed the ball back and forth away from me.

I moved to retrieve it but missed. "Give it back."

Ato laughed. "You must learn to protect the ball."

Derek walked up, distracting both of them. I jumped forward and got the ball but dropped all of my books. All three of them laughed.

Headmaster Quaye walked up. "What is happening here?"

Ato pointed at me. "Kwaku dropped his books trying to dribble."

"Kwaku, you shouldn't be playing football right now. You should be headed to class," Mr Quaye said, hands on his hips.

"Yes, sir," I responded, while staring at the other three boys. Ato and Edward angered me, but Derek's lack of defence for me, his own brother, left me dejected.

Their taunts and slight abuses continued for several days. Derek never participated directly, but he allowed it to happen. I did not tell my parents and hoped that he would eventually like me—even love me as his brother. The way Thomas and Bridget did.

* * *

Two days later, I dribbled my football to class, books in hand.

Thump!

Edward kicked my ball away while Ato knocked my books down. Several students laughed.

I clenched my fists. "Give it back!"

I moved to block the pass, but they managed to keep it from me twice before I intercepted it. I picked up the ball when Edward grabbed my arms from behind.

Edward was the same size and build as me, but Ato stood a head taller. I did not care about his size or being outnumbered. I was determined to fight for my ball—my pride.

Ato ripped the ball from me. "This is my ball now."

A large crowd gathered, forming a circle around the commotion. Ato looked around with a grin—perhaps proud of his accomplishment in obtaining the ball.

I stamped my foot down on Edward's shin.

"Owww!" he cried, and released my right arm.

I swung wildly at Ato catching the tip of his chin but doing no real damage. He dropped the ball and swung back striking my left eye. I fell to the ground taking Edward with me. Ato took a step towards me, fist raised.

"Quit it!"

We all looked at who barked that order. Derek stood there holding my ball.

"Quit it, Ato. Leave him alone." Derek remained firm.

Ato stepped towards Derek and pointed his finger at him. "I will do whatever I want, and there's nothing you can do to stop me."

Edward and I looked on, shocked by this turn of events.

Derek took a small step towards Ato, coming face-to-face. Ato grabbed the ball and turned his side to Derek.

"Ahhh!" Derek screamed, tackling Ato.

The ball flew into the growing crowd that had inched the circle tighter.

Ato and Derek rolled on the ground, wildly swinging at each other. Edward hopped up and attempted to pull Derek away, but I cut him off. We ended up a few feet away rolling around as well.

"Stop this!" Headmaster Quaye ran up. "You boys stop this right now!"

All four of us stopped fighting and looked up. Mr Quaye's booming voice commanded authority. "You four, come with me. The rest of you students, go to class."

Mr Quaye did not need to grab our shirt collars. We knew we were in trouble. We followed him as ordered.

Derek and I sat outside the Headmaster's office in the same chairs Daa and I sat in one week earlier. Mr Quaye called Ato and Edward into his office first, and although I could not understand what he was telling them, his raised voice likely meant a severe scolding.

I looked over at Derek through my right eye. The left one had not quite swollen shut, but everything appeared blurry through it. "Why did you defend me?"

He looked up, his bottom lip swollen—blood oozing out. "Because, you're my brother. Brothers look out for each other."

"But I thought you did not like me."

Derek lowered his head and looked down. "I'm sorry. I was just jealous at all the attention everyone gave you."

I smiled, and he looked up and smiled back. A pathetic sight we must have been with soiled clothes, scuffed elbows, and mangled faces. But inside, we were fine. We were brothers.

* * *

I thought of Mr Quaye as a fair man and hoped he knew that Ato and Edward started the fight. They left his office rubbing their buttocks and did not even look in our direction. Mr Quaye spared us that particular discipline and suggested we bring our problems to him next time. Headmaster Quaye said he would call our father and let him decide our punishment.

We walked towards Daa's car after school, uncertain of our fate.

Georgina, the girl who sat next to me in Mrs Mantey's class, walked up. "Kwaku! Want your ball?" She brought it from around her back and tossed it to me.

"Thank you," I said, eyes raised.

"Oh. Does your eye hurt?" She lifted her hand as if she were going to touch it.

I leaned back a bit. "No. I am fine."

"You better put some ice on it."

"I'm all right. Thank you for your concern," Kwaku said sarcastically—eye still swollen.

Georgina smiled and walked away.

"I think she likes you," Derek said.

I looked back at her with a slight grin.

"Derek. Kwaku. Come here." Daa's tone implied he was none too pleased.

I assumed a punishment awaited Derek and me, but I did not care. I gained a new brother. A great day indeed.

* * *

I managed to avoid Ato and Edward for the next several weeks; Derek had completely severed ties with them.

I spent every spare moment reading. I loved that school, and fortunately, had some great teachers. My grades suffered at first having missed a year of school. However, I improved over time.

I cautiously approached Daa in the living room.

"Daa, remember that you said if my grades were good at the end of term, I could play football?"

Daa looked up from his book. "I believe I said if your grades are exemplary by the end of term, you may play. Not simply good." He held out his hand. "I trust you received your report card?"

I held it behind my back, unsure what he considered exemplary.

He examined the document. "Mathematics - B. English - A. Social Studies - A. Science - B. French - C." He took off his reading glasses and looked up at me. "Would you consider these grades exemplary or good?"

I looked down at the ground, arms folded. I knew the grades did not rate anything special. "Just good, I suppose."

"Well, Kwaku, in my opinion, these are exemplary grades for someone who missed a year of schooling. I'm very proud of you."

I looked up, mouth open, more surprised than happy.

"Now, we will certainly want you to get these grades up as you progress. I want you to strive for all A's."

I nodded. "I am worried about French. I do not understand so much of it. I get confused."

"I have it on good authority that an excellent French tutor lives under this roof. Did you know that your Ma is fluent in French? I am sure she will be happy to help."

"And football?"

"You may play football, as long as you maintain your grades and work to improve them. I'll call the football coach, tout de suite."

I cocked my head. "Toot sweet?"

* * *

I stepped on to the Achimota School football pitch with the required jersey and a used pair of boots. I had never worn boots and hoped they would present no challenges.

I had always played in my bare feet in the past. Everyone turned and looked at me. I knew several of the players but none of them had become my friends.

Ato and Edward stood on the pitch staring at me along with the rest of the players. Several kicked the ball around near the sidelines waiting to start practice. Ato grinned and slightly shook his head—I suppose disapproving of my arrival. Edward gave me a slight wave. He had approached me one week after the altercation and said he was sorry, but we had not spoken since.

Coach Addo cleared his throat. "Listen up. We have a new player trying out today. This is Kwaku. We will see if he can play."

Daa told me that Coach Addo had played on a victorious Africa Cup of Nations Team several years before.

I offered a weak wave to the other players.

The pitch could not have seemed more different from the one I played on in the fishing village. The Achimota School pitch certainly did not meet World Cup standards, but at least it was flat. Proper white goals with nets stood at each end and chalk lightly defined the edges of the field. Rather than dirt, grass covered much of the field, and I saw no rocks for me to avoid.

I had played a casual game or two in the last few months with my brothers, but experienced no competition since those days in the fishing village. Those opponents were mere fisher boys like me. Coach Addo ran us through several drills. My pinpoint accuracy with the ball had left me. Footballs flew left of the goal, right of the goal, and over the goal.

"I thought you could play football, Kwaku," Ato said. He approached a placed ball and shot it sharply in the corner of the goal. "You see, that is how you shoot a football."

We divided up for a scrimmage. My ability to stop the ball and dribble matched the other boys on the team. On three occasions, however, I had opportunities to score and missed the goal each time.

Ato elbowed a player next to him. "Kwaku plays fishing village style. No goals. They shoot it and think they scored a goal." The comment earned a few chuckles.

I walked off the pitch at the end of practice, head hung low.

Ato delivered one more mocking comment. "Orphan boys don't belong here. You don't belong here. You should go back to fishing."

Every ounce of me wanted to fight him. I reared my arm back, fist clenched.

"Kwaku, come here," Coach Addo said.

I ran up to the coach worried he would tell me not to come back.

"Your dribbling is excellent. You move the ball well. However, your kicking leaves much to be desired. I assume you have not played in awhile so you may need some extra practice. Can you do that?"

"Yes, sir."

"I have many good players on my team. Many good dribblers. But I need forwards. Solid strikers."

* * *

Dissatisfied with my performance, I asked Daa to bring me to school early the next morning so I could practise. I wore my school uniform but put on the boots. Derek and Thomas stood by the goal and rolled the ball back after each shot. After twenty minutes of this frustration, Coach Addo walked onto the pitch.

"I see you are practising very hard, but without much improvement."

I shook my head. "I do not understand. I used to be able to shoot the ball exactly where I wanted."

"Did you wear boots or shoes of any kind when you played before?"

"No, Coach. Just my bare feet."

He pointed to my feet. "Take them off. And the socks."

I looked at him, confused, but did as instructed.

"Now, try again."

The first three balls landed in the goal. Coach Addo began calling out spots where he wanted me to shoot the ball. Nine of ten hit their mark.

"Well now. You can shoot. But we have a problem, don't we? You cannot play a match in bare feet."

I looked down at my feet and rolled back and forth on them. "What can I do?"

"When you kick the ball, what do you think about?"

"Where I want the ball to go?"

"Yes, but break down the thought process even more. What do you think when your foot kicks the ball?" Coach Addo held up his foot and slapped it. "At the exact moment your foot touches it?"

I looked off to the side considering this. I had never thought that much about it. "I suppose I think about the exact part of foot I want to use. And how hard to kick it."

"That's right. Now when you wear boots, what do you think about?"

"The boot. The whole boot."

He smiled. "And now we have found the problem. With boots on, you are not focused on the exact location of your foot. You are thinking about the whole boot, am I correct?"

"Yes. Yes, that is it."

"So put your boots back on. And then forget them. When you kick, only think about your bare foot and the exact point you will use to kick."

* * *

My jersey fit perfectly; my boots as well. I stood with my teammates for my first match on a real team. Daa, Ma, and my sister and brothers sat in the stands ready to cheer us on. I wanted to get down on my hands and knees and smell the grass. To enjoy every moment.

A mere five months earlier, I fished for Ben all day and into the night. Those days were gone. My new life had come.

I had practised with the team for two weeks. Since I came to the team late, Coach Addo had held me out of the first match a week prior. My confidence level suffered a bit knowing that so many teammates depended on me.

What if I let them down? What if I make a mistake?

Daa had told me to "do my best and leave the results to God." Wise words I suppose but they failed to relieve the nerves in my stomach.

Ato played centre forward—our main striker. I played left forward. I had no reason to like Ato. He never acknowledged me as a teammate or offered a word of encouragement. He had even deliberately tripped me—or at least I think it was deliberate—during one of our practice sessions. However, I must admit he played the game very well—a superb striker. I was sure that once we played in an actual match, he would work with me. Work in unison towards victory.

By half-time, we managed to keep the score at 1-1, with Ato scoring a goal for our team.

My nerves had calmed and I settled for the second half, ready to contribute. The other team's defender managed to cover me very well whenever I reached a scoring position. I struggled with him late into the second half. The opposing team scored, leading 2-1 with only a few minutes left in the match.

Our goalie stopped another potential goal and kicked the ball far down the field. One of our midfielders passed the ball to Ato. Two defenders closed in on him.

I had been making the same move towards the goal every time we had the ball close to scoring position. I always ran straight towards the goal, almost to the point of being offside if I had outrun the defender and had the ball played to me.

This time, I faked a move towards the goal, then ran horizontal to the goal and towards Ato. The defender fell down attempting to correct himself when he noticed he ran the wrong way. I managed to create an enormous space between the goal and me. I held up my hand and Ato looked right at me. He had plenty of room to pass me the ball.

"Ato! Pass!" I yelled, now jumping up in the air.

For almost three seconds, Ato could have passed. But he did not. He started to turn and clumsily tried to pass the ball back to our midfielder. By that time, the other team's defenders caught up with him, and reclaimed the ball. They managed to fend off our attack. The referee blew the whistle, ending the game.

I stared at Ato, my hands up in the air.

Coach Addo gathered us together.

He placed his hands on his hips. "Ato, why didn't you pass the ball to Kwaku? He was open. He could easily have scored."

Ato pointed at me and stared—hate in his eyes. "He was offside. It wouldn't have counted."

The coach shook his head. "No, Ato. He was not offside. The defender was clearly lying on the ground forward of him."

We all remained silent. Several stared at Ato.

"Listen up," Coach Addo said, clearing his throat and pacing back and forth. "No one person on this team is more important than another. No one person can win by himself. We are a team and we have to work together. We win together. We lose together. Does everyone understand?"

"Yes, sir!" several shouted. Except Ato. He remained silent. Defiant.

I resolved to be a team player. To pass the ball when needed. To score the goal when needed. I resolved that I would be a great football player, but only as a member of a unified team.

FOURTEEN

Six years later, I held my university identification card. Although I did not much care for my photograph, I proudly showed the card whenever an opportunity arose. It meant I belonged. That I deserved to be there. The black star on the Ghanaian flag stood as a reminder that we are all Africans—of our unity. I was always African, and Ghanaian. But now also a member of a grand university.

Through focused study, lots of help from teachers, and the constant reading of books, I earned excellent grades and graduated senior high school number two in my class; Georgina earned the number one spot. Daa urged me to attend his alma mater, the University of Ghana-Legon.

I considered many fields of study such as economics and classics, but eventually settled on history. I had a passion for all fields of history, but modern Europe intrigued me the most. I suppose it stemmed from Daa's constant diatribes about the state of Europe.

"Did you hear what the prime minister is proposing?" Or "During the Victorian era . . . " he would say.

Collegiate studies presented many challenges, but I embraced the work. I loved the lively classroom discussions, especially history and politics. I managed to continue my academic success from senior high school throughout my first two years at the university.

My life during this time contained one major distraction, a young lady, Grace, that I met in my literature class. We met on the first day of class in my second year. Running a bit late, I clumsily fell into an open seat and dropped my books. While retrieving them from the floor, I heard a voice.

"I believe this is your pencil."

I looked up, mouth wide-open. There were many appropriate responses I could have given, such as a simple thank you, but none came to mind. I stared back and slowly nodded, receiving the pencil.

"You're welcome," she said.

I nodded again. Still no verbal reply from me. I sat dumbfounded and amazed at her beauty. She was beautiful from the side, but when she turned and smiled at me, everything else in the universe ceased.

She listened to the lecture and took notes. Thirty minutes passed and I had failed to write a single note. I kept thinking about her and stole a glance every few minutes.

"Kwaku, will you read Tennyson for us?" said a voice that barely registered.

I stared towards the ground, still lost in thought.

"Kwaku? Kwaku?"

"Yes," I responded. I looked around and everyone stared back. The professor held her book to her chest and stared at me.

"Can you read *The Charge of the Light Brigade*? Page 231."

"Uh . . . yes, Ma'am." I quickly flipped to the page and began reading the iconic poem.

I hid my attraction from Grace for several weeks before mustering the courage to ask her on a date. We had had some brief conversations in the past. Most of them pointless, where I came up with some excuse to talk with her. An upcoming football match between some local teams presented an opportunity.

We began to gather our things at the end of literature class. I looked around to make sure no one else could hear.

"Ahem. Grace. Do you like football?"

"Not really. My brothers are obsessed with it and it's all they talk about."

My master plan fell apart before it started. I had no alternate plan. No idea how to salvage this disaster.

She began walking away.

Sensing defeat, I offered the proposal anyway.

"Oh. Well, there is a local match this Saturday. I thought you might like to go. But I suppose not since you do not like football."

That was stupid. Why would I have asked her, then give her a reason to say no? I typically spoke with confidence. But not with Grace.

She put her hands on her hips. "Well, I thought you meant discussing football. I don't care to discuss it that much, but I do like to watch. I'd love to go with you."

"Great! See you then." Thrilled, I began walking away.

"Kwaku. Aren't you going to tell me where to meet? What time?"

All legitimate questions for a rational person, but I was far too smitten.

* * *

I suppose some would call football a distraction, but I managed to play the game and maintain my studies. My football mentor, Coach Addo, steered me towards a local club, Legon United FC.

As I approached the halfway point of my time at the university, next year's World Cup loomed over all of us. No one suggested the Ghana Black Stars as favourites to win, but they seemed one of the best teams Africa had to offer.

Like most Ghanaian boys, I dreamt of playing for the Black Stars. Any football player hopes to reach the pinnacle of their sport. Legon United FC used me as their main striker—affording me the opportunity to score many goals. And I scored many, benefiting from a unified team that worked well together in setting up goal-scoring opportunities.

The football would sometimes appear to me in slow motion. In the heat of a game, with defenders surrounding me, everything slowed down. I could see the type of spin on the ball offering me the advantage of kicking it at just the right point. A God-given instinct, I suppose. My shot accuracy only improved over time.

During practice one day, I noticed a man talking with our coach. They called me over.

"Kwaku, I'd like you to meet James Ofori. He is the coach of—"

I cut him off. "The Black Stars." I, of course, knew Coach Ofori. Everyone knew him.

Coach Ofori extended his hand. "Kwaku. I am sure you follow the Black Stars and have heard we've experienced some unfortunate injuries to several of our forwards—players that are unbelievable strikers."

I wiped the sweat from my brow. "Yes, sir. I hope you find some good replacements. I think the Black Stars will be the hope of Africa in this World Cup."

The coaches looked at each other and smiled.

"Why do you think I'm here?" Coach Ofori said. "I want you to play with us."

I should have offered some response, but much like the time with Grace, I was speechless.

"Well, Kwaku, what do you say?"

I nodded and reached to shake his hand. "Uh . . . yes. Yes, of course!"

Coach Ofori folded his arms and lowered his head. "Now, listen. That doesn't mean you will play in the matches. We have players with far more experience. Players that have U-20 and Ghana Premier League experience serving as backups. Coach Addo told me about you so I watched a couple of your matches. You have a raw talent unlike any I have seen in many years. So, you have potential. You will be there in case of emergency. Some of the players may resent an unproven player in a Black Star jersey. Can you handle that?"

"Yes, sir. I am ready."

"This means you may miss some school. But this is an once-in-a-lifetime opportunity."

* * *

"You are going to drop out of the university over football?" Ma did not receive the news as well as the rest of the family. They expressed their congratulations, but Ma took a more practical stance.

I rolled my eyes. "No, Ma. Not dropping out. It is a leave of . . . of—"

"Absence. A short leave of absence," Daa said, and then held up a finger. "It's a once-in-a-lifetime opportunity. Don't worry. I will make sure he misses no more school than required for these trips."

Ma placed her hand on her hips. "Well, I can see by the smiles on all of these faces that it is five against one. I suppose we better pray for you."

* * *

My national team experience would certainly go down in history as different from most. I was no Abedi Pele. As Coach Ofori had said, I did not have the experience of most other players on the team. Seven had played in the World Cup before. Three had come from their English

Premier League teams. Many of them had played in the Africa Cup of Nations.

"Hey, Legon team boy. Fetch me some water," was a common type of disrespectful comment I would receive from the senior players. They were never mean, just dismissive of me. They probably assumed I would last only a week. But over time, I earned my spot on the team in practice. I never relented in the drills. If we ran, I ran faster. If we shot the ball, I was more accurate. But I understood that it took more than physical talent to win the World Cup. It took experience. I had only played against other Ghanaians. But now I would play against other Africans, Europeans, North Americans, and South Americans.

Many sports writers assumed one or two African teams would make it through the early rounds. A team like Cameroon perhaps, but not Ghana. Europe's top teams would likely comprise those left in the quarterfinals with Germany, the likely champion.

I played a few minutes in the final qualifying match to give the starting players rest. The sheer magnitude of this stage was not lost on me, but I shut that out of my mind and only considered the field of play. The pitch and number of players were no different from any match I had played in the last few years. I touched the ball only twice, both times passing back to a defender. We had the match won and only needed to keep the ball away from the other team.

"Kwaku, you played well, " Arthur Asare said, an experienced player who mentored me on being a Black Star.

We began walking towards the locker room. "Thank you, but I did not do very much."

He held up a finger much the way Daa had done many times. "Not true. You are a team player. Your foot skills kept the ball away from the other team. You had a job to do in those final minutes and you did it. That is all we can ask."

"I know my place is to back up the starting line-up, but I would be very happy if I played more."

Arthur smiled. "Everyone wants to play. Coach Ofori has a keen eye for talent. You would not be here if he thought you couldn't contribute. And I don't mean keeping the bench warm. I mean playing—scoring. You're going to England with us. You are a Black Star."

There are few times in my life I would define as seminal moments, but that was one. That was the first time I truly felt like a Black Star.

* * *

"I am so jealous. You are going to England. I've always wanted to go there," Derek said, twirling my football while sitting on my bed.

I inspected the empty suitcase and contemplated my packing list. "Two more days and I am off."

"You must bring me back a souvenir. One of those shirts with a British flag. What do you call it? The Union something?"

I smiled. "Yes, the Union Jack. I will if I have time. You do know I will be there to play in the World—"

Bridget burst into our room. "You must come quickly. Daa fainted at his office."

* * *

We waited for two hours at the hospital for some answer. Bridget sat next to Ma rubbing her back. Derek stared out of the window. Thomas and I paced back and forth in the hallway. Hospital staff busied themselves with their work. I noticed the occasional glance from strangers, no doubt waiting to hear the fate of their loved ones. White walls and white floors offered no sense of consolation, but rather blankness and nothingness.

"Kwaku, I came as soon as I could," Grace said, offering me a comforting hug. "How is he?"

"We do not know; they have not told us anything yet."

I could think only of losing my biological father and mother. I could not bear losing another parent.

A doctor in a white coat and stethoscope around his neck came to our end of the hallway. He looked down at his clipboard. "Mrs Boateng?"

Ma stood and nodded.

"I'm afraid your husband is suffering from a severe case of malaria. He is resting now and you can see him. But not all at once."

"How severe? Will he be all right?" Bridget asked.

"I honestly do not know. These things have to run their course. He's very weak."

Ma and Bridget went into Daa's room.

Grace held my hand as we walked down the hall waiting for my turn. "He is in God's hands," she said.

I pulled my hand away. "God's hands. My father and mother were in God's hands. Prince was in God's hands. And they were all taken away from me."

"You must have faith, Kwaku. Faith that God knows what is best for your father. For you. For all of us."

I shook my head and then stared at the wall.

"Look at me." She put her hand under my chin. "Look at me."

I gave in and looked back.

"How many times have you said the same thing to me? Not two weeks ago at church when we prayed for that sick little girl. What did you say? You said she was in God's hands. So it is with that little girl and so it is with your father."

"I know."

"What was it your biological father used to tell you? 'Always look for God.' I am sure he meant that in good times and bad times."

I nodded.

"Kwaku, I know you've experienced so much pain in your life. But now is when you must be strong. You need to be strong for your father. Now is when you rely on your faith in God more than ever. Show your father that when you go in to see him, and I will pray."

"I love you, Grace."

"Of course you do. Who wouldn't?"

Grace always knew how to make me smile.

Daa lay in bed, eyes barely open. My brothers joined me around Daa's bed.

He offered a smile and whispered. "You boys be strong for Ma and Bridget. They need you now more than ever."

A tear rolled down Derek's cheek.

"Don't worry about me. Pray often, but do not worry. We will trust God." Daa coughed and readjusted himself in the bed. "Kwaku, you have a big trip. I wish I could be there in person."

"I am not going."

Thomas and Derek jerked their heads in my direction.

"I cannot leave while you are sick. I need to be here."

Daa curled his finger, motioning for me to come closer. "No. You go. You must go."

I shook my head. "My place is with my family."

"Listen," Daa said.

I readied for one of his famous speeches. He had one for every situation.

"There is nothing you can do sitting around here or at home. The most important thing you can do is to pray. And you can do that anywhere. You must go and you must play. You are representing Ghana. You are representing Africa, and more importantly, you are representing the God Most High. You are his witness in Accra, and Africa, and England. You go and play for him. And when anyone asks you about your football, you tell them you do it all for God's glory."

FIFTEEN

I loved England, Buckingham Palace, Westminster Abbey, and Big Ben. We rode the red double-decker buses throughout the city between our training and matches. We had runs through Hyde Park. While not much of a tea drinker before, I became accustomed to a spot of tea every afternoon. And I really liked the people.

A lady named Mrs Blair cared for us in our little hotel. Every evening she would say, "If you chaps need anything, let me know." She became our mother while in London.

Most assumed the Ghana Black Stars would return home soon—losing in the early rounds. But we played with intensity. We beat teams such as Chile, France, and Cameroon on our way to the semifinals. Germany solidified their spot in the final with a 3-1 win over England, the home team. Brazil—the previous World Cup champion—stood in our way to the final.

I played more in the last several games due to fatigued and injured players. The experience gave me more confidence. I desperately wanted more playing time, but knew my place.

Arthur, our team captain, grabbed my arm on the way out of the locker room to face Brazil. "Listen, Kwaku. I'm

144

certain we'll need you today. Be ready to play. Be ready to score. OK?"

I nodded. I was ready.

Beautiful weather met us for the semifinal. The Brazilian team marched on the field, heads held high. Not in a cocky sense, but with the confidence that came from their recent success on the international stage. We maintained a healthy respect for their accomplishments but knew that our best play could beat them.

I watched the first half from the bench. Our team played well but were down 1-0 at halftime.

Coach Ofori gathered us before we walked out for the second half. "We've played well, but we could be up 3-1. Too many scoring opportunities missed." He turned to me. "Kwaku."

I looked up. Why would he call my name?

"You're starting at centre forward in the second half. I'll expect you to take the shots we set up. I'll expect you to produce goals."

I stood up. "Yes, sir!"

"Brazil's defenders will play your teammates closer than they will with you, Kwaku, likely assuming you're not a threat." Coach Ofori spanned the room. "That's our advantage. Feed Kwaku the ball."

I touched the ball several times in the first twenty minutes of the half with no opportunities to score. Finally, I had the ball on a run with no obstacle but the goalie. I shot hard to the top right corner. The goalie made a good jump, diverting the ball with the tips of his fingers, and causing it to veer past the upright.

"Awww!" roared the crowd.

The majority of the fans seemed to cheer for Brazil, but I heard enough cheers for us to know we had fans.

One of Brazil's defenders headed the corner kick out to a teammate. The momentum forced several of their players away from our goal, but Arthur intercepted the ball and passed it to me in stride from the right of the pitch. With a defender in front of me, I dribbled behind, my left foot creating a clear path to the goal. I shoot better with my right foot but had scored a third of my goals in the past with my left. The goalie made a slight move to his left, centering himself in front of the goal. I shot it hard to the left and raised my hands before the ball touched the back of the net.

Goal!

Teammates surrounded me. One thought entered my mind. I specifically remembered a time on Lake Volta pulling in a net. I imagined myself scoring a goal for the Black Stars in the World Cup. A fisherboy's dream had become reality.

With time about to expire, we remained deadlocked at 1-1. Brazil had excelled that year at scoring last-minute goals—adept at the knockout punch.

My third scoring opportunity occurred on a corner kick. The ball sailed in past the far end of the goal, and I tapped it towards the goal. The goalie had remained on the nearer end to the corner kick. The tap would easily have scored over the right shoulder of a defender to give us a 2-1 advantage. However, the defender raised his right hand blocking the goal.

The foul earned us a penalty kick, and Coach Ofori signalled for me to take it. I stared at the goalie for several seconds. Even with the roaring crowd, I shut out all outside interference. I heard and felt nothing. I looked down at the ball, wiping sweat from the sides of my face.

All for your glory, Lord.

I glanced at the left side of the goal and looked back down quickly. My body and left foot planted, leaning to the left side. The goalie moved to his right. I shot the ball the opposite way of all that momentum. It powered in the top right of the net. Goal!

This time I did not raise my hands. I stood there and smiled. Arthur ran towards me and picked me up.

With under a minute remaining, we strategically kept the ball away from Brazil. The referee allowed extra time but blew the whistle after three minutes. The crowd erupted. We gathered at midfield jumping up and down and hugging.

We made it. We made the finals.

* * *

Daa left the hospital after six long days. He stayed in bed at home for two more weeks but eventually regained his strength. Thomas and Derek had moved our one television into his bedroom so he could watch the matches.

I sat on my hotel room bed and dialled the long-distance number to talk with him before the final. "Daa, how are you feeling?"

"I am well, Kwaku. I've even returned to work. But, I believe it is football that made me well, ha-ha."

147

"Football, why football?"

"Of course the Great Physician has made me well, but I was determined to see you play in the World Cup. I've watched every match they've broadcasted and now you're in the finals. Are you ready?"

"I think so. But have you seen the papers? They say things like 'Germany will crush Ghana,' and 'Ghana's miracle season is over.'"

"Yes, Kwaku, I've read those things. But those sports writers have nothing to do with play on the pitch. They have nothing to do with your feet. They have nothing to do with your will to win. I'm making my own prediction. I'm predicting a victory for Ghana."

* * *

Arthur grabbed me as we walked into the stadium, much as he did before the Brazil match. "No pressure, Kwaku. But I need you to score five goals today."

I stopped walking and looked back at him. "Five goals?"

He smiled. "OK, maybe four goals."

Getting the joke, I smiled and nodded as we kept walking.

"Kwaku, God has given you an amazing talent. Let him work through you today. Do your best and leave the results to God."

A sea of faces greeted us as we marched onto the pitch. I turned in circles to take them all in. Several flags flew at one end of the stadium revealing a slight wind. The grass smelled newly cut with fresh chalk lines—ready for action.

This match presented the most physical challenge I had experienced in my short career. The defenders grabbed and bumped me at every opportunity. In particular, Germany's Rolf Schroeder tried to inflict a little pain at every point of contact. He had a reputation as a dirty player. His biceps practically burst out of his shirtsleeves, the veins running over enormous muscles. He included verbal jabs as well.

"Is this your best?" or "you'll never beat us," and others that do not bear repeating.

I scored early with a header from a corner kick and Arthur scored a brilliant goal past two defenders giving us a 2-2 tie.

My battles with Schroeder took their toll on my body. No fewer than three times he rammed my left leg, and in particular my left knee. The swelling required icing at halftime.

"Can you keep playing, Kwaku?" Coach Ofori asked.

"Absolutely! I am ready."

We remained deadlocked for the most of the second half. Great defence by both teams with few shots on goal. As we approached the final minutes, Schroeder came down hard on my left knee. I rolled on the pitch, holding my knee, and wincing in pain.

The referee showed the big German a yellow card.

Schroeder stretched out his arms and open palms. "I was going for the ball. He stuck his leg out to block me."

The referee ignored his pleas. How he had managed to avoid a yellow card up to this point defies explanation.

Play resumed with the ball going back and forth over midfield as we entered extra time. My knee throbbed and weighed me down. Every time I put weight on it, a sharp pain ran up my thigh. I put it out of my mind.

"Ole . . . ole-ole-ole!" chants came from the crowd.

Arthur stole the ball from a German midfielder and dribbled towards the centre of the goal. With my bad knee, I could not outrun the defender closest to me, so I ran with him, managing to keep myself between him and the ball. Arthur passed it to me as I came close to the penalty box. Schroeder moved from the back of the penalty box towards me. The goalie bent down, arms outstretched, ready to block my shot.

The ball bounced a few feet from me. I planted on my left foot. Pain shot up my thigh. The defender hooked his right arm under my left. Schroeder scowled, ready to pounce.

Then, as I had noticed in one of those first days of playing in the fishing village, the ball hovered in midair, as if in slow motion. The ball had no spin. The world stopped.

The defender pulled down on my left arm. I put my right instep under it with barely a tap, and just enough to redirect it.

The ball floated over Schroeder's left shoulder—his eyes following it all the way. The goalie jumped towards the top corner—the ball passing within inches of his fingers.

No power. All finesse. Goal!

The crowd erupted. My teammates tackled me. Schroeder dropped his head and put his hands on his hips.

I limped towards midfield. Play resumed but ended within one minute.

The crowd shouted, repeatedly, "Black Stars! Black Stars! Black Stars!"

My teammates tackled me. I lay there crushed under the pile and enjoyed every second of it.

I looked forward to the eventual headlines: 'Ghana defeats Germany' or 'Ghana: World Cup Champions'.

Several reporters cornered me, shoving microphones and recording devices in my face. No one had ever interviewed me before.

"Ghansah, how does it feel to be a World Cup Champion?" one reporter asked.

I must have looked ridiculous standing there with a large grin on my face, non-responsive. I finally offered up a trite response. "Uh . . . good. Great. Wonderful."

Another reporter leaned in. "Kwaku, how did you do it? How did you score the winning goal?"

I prepared to offer a generic football response, but thought the better of it. "I can only think of one thing. God gave me the talent. It is all for God's glory." My grin subsided. I made no expression. "And one other thing. I dedicate that goal to my friend Prince, the bravest person I ever knew. To his memory."

* * *

Ghana held a parade and celebration for us at Black Star Square in Accra. Thousands attended with cheers and shouts. Unfortunately, I had trouble navigating through the crowds on crutches. My knee injury had been worse than first thought.

151

The crowds slowly left. Grace and my family joined me as we began to leave.

"Kwaku."

I stopped my waddle. I had heard my name called hundreds of times that day. This one sounded distinctly different. I knew that voice. A voice I had not heard in years. I turned.

She stood there, frail and gaunt. "Kwaku, it's me."

"Mercy? Mercy, is that you?"

Ma walked up behind me and put her hands on my shoulders. "Is this your sister?"

I nodded, slowly.

No other words were needed. We both cried and embraced for what seemed several minutes.

"Well, Kwaku, aren't you going to introduce us?" Ma asked.

After the introductions, Daa cleared his throat. "Mercy, we have a little family celebration planned at our home. I can think of no better guest than you to join us."

She looked around as if looking for someone's permission. "Uh…yes…thank you, sir."

We piled in Daa's car making for a tight fit.

"I have so many questions to ask. Where have you been? Where do you live? I bet you want to know the same about me. I—"

Mercy held up her hand. "Please, Kwaku. Maybe we can talk more when we get to your home."

I thought this strange. Mercy never shied from conversation before. She seemed uncomfortable and anxious. She looked over her shoulder and out the back window.

Daa looked at us through the rearview mirror. "Kwaku, you must be exhausted. Perhaps you can talk more at home."

I then understood what Daa had already figured out. Mercy wanted to talk in private.

* * *

With full bellies, Mercy and I sat on the back patio— just the two of us. I proceeded to tell her everything that happened to me. Simon selling me to Master Ben, the fishing, the beatings, and the murder of Prince. I told her of the adoption, school, and all of it.

She wiped her tears.

I put my hand on top of hers. "So, it's been seven long years. I thought of you every day. I have prayed for you. The second day I came to this house, Daa took me to Agbogbloshie to find you. We looked all day. Even talking to Auntie Agnes. I chased a woman through the streets, because I thought she was you. We returned many times, but could not find you."

Mercy sniffed and sat back in her chair. "That Auntie Agnes is an evil woman. She forced me to do horrible things. Selling my body. I hate her."

I did not know what to say.

Mercy looked off into the distance for several seconds, and then continued. "The day you did not come back to the shanty, I asked her where you were. She said you probably ran off, and that I should forget about you. I protested and said I needed to find you. She slapped me and sent me back out to work. But, I didn't go to work. I looked for you for two days. One of the men who worked for Auntie Agnes found me and dragged me back to the shanty. He beat me and—"

She covered her hand with her mouth and began crying again.

"He, what?"

"He beat me. He said Auntie Agnes told him to punish me. My body ached and my face took weeks to heal. As soon as it did, she sold me to another man who forced me to work. Then, that man sold me. This went on for a year. I wanted to leave Agbogbloshie, but worried I would never find you if I left. So I stayed for two more years."

"I am so sorry, Mercy. I wish you would have left right away."

"I finally decided that you were not coming back. And that I'd rather starve than keep doing that work for a master and suffer the constant beatings for not earning enough money. One day, I ran away."

I leaned towards her. "Where did you go?"

"Many places in Accra. Anywhere I could find shelter. I found some work in hotels. I carried a head tray and sold in the streets, around Osu. Mostly, I do the work I know best, but I am my own boss." She leaned towards me, resolute. "I work when I want with who I want."

"Mercy. You do not have to do that work any longer. I will take care of you. My family will take care of you."

"No. I don't need anyone to take care of me. I don't need a boss. I don't need charity. I make my own way. I have my own shanty near Oxford Street."

Mercy began to act anxious again. Looking around and rubbing her arms. "Those men I used to work for are still looking for me. I know they are. But I will not let them get me."

"Mercy, let me help you."

She stood up. "No!" she said, loudly.

The rest of the family looked at us through the window.

Mercy closed her eyes while lowering her head. She took a step towards me, opening her eyes. "Kwaku, I know you are trying to help. But . . . but you have a different life now. I've read about you in the newspapers. I heard about this young player named Stephen Ghansah on the Black Stars." She smiled. "It wasn't until I saw your picture that I knew it was you. You look just like our father. I'm proud of you. You have so much to live for. You shouldn't be involved with someone like me. You have a future. I'm a nobody. Just forget about me."

"Mercy, you are my sister. My future is with you. God has brought us back together. Remember what Father always said. 'Always look for God.'"

"God gave up on me a long time ago, Kwaku."

"Do not say that, Mercy. Let me—"

"I have to go, Kwaku. I have to work. I will call you."

Mercy moved through the house, quickly. "Mr and Mrs Boateng, thank you for the meal."

And just like that, she was gone from my life. Again.

SIXTEEN

Shortly after Mercy left, the day of the parade, I told my family her story. All of them wanted to help, but Bridget made it her life's mission. It took several months, but she found her shanty. Mercy shunned her initially, but Bridget kept at her. My sister Bridget is the most persistent person I have ever known. If she becomes determined to do something, it will get done. Her persistence convinced Daa and Ma to adopt me.

Bridget convinced Mercy to attend our church. She became a regular attender and found work as a waitress in a hotel restaurant. It took her a few years to stop looking over her shoulder and believe that no masters sought after her.

Although a grown woman, Daa and Ma adopted Mercy. They did not need to go through the Department of Social Welfare or complete any paper work since she was an adult. Some might call it symbolic. For Mercy, it meant a God-ordained family, a sister, more brothers, in-laws for a future spouse, and grandparents for future children.

Many assumed that I would make football a career. Unfortunately, my knee injury in the World Cup was only a symptom of lingering issues with both of my knees. Doctors told me I required surgery on my left knee immediately to keep playing, and I would likely suffer continuous knee injuries. After much prayer and consultation, I decided that I had lived my football dream and wanted to move on to other things. I would always be able to play casually, but not at the professional level.

I continued my studies at the university. Although majoring in history, I closely followed politics and government, engaging in various debates and discussions on the issues of the day.

I adored the Ghanaian national anthem—especially the line that read, "The cause of freedom and of right." I suppose it became sort of a life motto for me. After graduation from college, Harvard University offered me a scholarship in their graduate school. I spent two years in the United States earning a Masters in Public Policy and planned to use that degree in aiding the cause of freedom and of right. Four years after my World Cup experience, I settled into a teaching position at the university in Legon.

My family endured many of my political rants. "Ghana must change the way it relates to businesses. We must—Why are you laughing?" I said, noticing Bridget's chuckling.

"Kwaku, you had your finger in the air like Daa. Just like one of his famous lectures." She wagged her finger in the air to mock me.

Daa chimed in. "No politics today, Kwaku. We are focused on kingdom work. We are headed to the fishing village where we found you."

I had enjoyed many evangelism trips before, but this would be my first time back there. I had always declined in the past, having too many bad memories. I had no idea whether I would find this difficult or liberating, but I wanted to face the challenge.

We parked in the heart of the village and Daa greeted an older man there, the pastor of the church. Daa seemed to know at least one person in every village.

I noticed the smell of the lake before anything else. Instantly, memories of fishing entered my mind. It did not upset me, but reminded me of the backbreaking work.

Bridget always carried a jug of water and paper cups to share with anyone desiring a drink of cold water. It was her way of living out Jesus' words in the book of Matthew about giving a cup of cold water to little ones. She used me for her jug carrier. We headed down the road while Daa continued his conversation.

Several children stopped their play in the street for a drink from us. They wore few clothes and most ran in bare feet. People walked back and forth, busy with their day. A few men sat next to a building, appearing to do nothing close to work. We knew from past experience that sharing the Gospel to drunken people produced little fruit. We continued on our way, walking past an alley.

"Hey. You, boy," cough. Cough.

The voice caused me to stop. A haunting voice. Urine almost ran down my leg.

"Hey, boy. Give me water." Master Ben lay in the alley, one eye barely open.

I approached him slowly. "Ben?"

He held onto an empty bottle of alcohol. "What? How do you know my name, boy?" his speech slurred.

Bridget stood behind me but said nothing.

I knelt down by him. "It is me, Kwaku. Do you remember me?"

"Who?"

"Kwaku. I was your slave many years ago. Me and a boy named Prince."

He quickly looked up when I said Prince. I knew that he remembered.

"I don't remember no boy named Prince. Or you."

"Bridget, let me have a cup."

I poured some water and gave it to Ben, but I really wanted to strangle him. I wanted to make him pay for what he did to Prince, Ivy, and me. I wanted to bring him to justice. He laid there, a pathetic shell of the man I remembered. He looked like an old man but was probably only 40 years old. A drunk.

I wanted to hurt him, but remembered God's word that, "Vengeance is mine."

"Ben, you need help. You need food. You need shelter. But most importantly, you need Jesus."

The pastor and Daa walked up, and Bridget whispered to them.

Daa opened his mouth in disbelief. "Ben?"

"You know old Ben here?" the pastor said.

Daa nodded. "Yes. This is the man who forced Kwaku to fish."

"Oh, I see. Ben here lost his business to drunkenness. I have tried to get him to come to church many times. Isn't that right, Ben?" the pastor said.

Ben looked up, one eye closed and one open, at our conversation and then looked away at the pastor's comments. I could tell it bothered him. Hating Ben would do no one any good. Ignoring him would do no good.

"Ben. I know that you know who I am. I know you remember Prince and Ivy. And I know you remember John, William, and Lionel. I know you remember the way you treated us. I know you remember what you did to Prince. I want you to know that God will forgive you if you repent. He knows your heart. I forgive you. Turn your life over to Christ. He can redeem all of it. He can make you a new creation. It is never too late to turn your life over to God."

Ben had looked away from me the whole time. He turned back towards me. A tear rolled down his cheek. He said nothing. I did not expect him to. I touched his shoulder and walked away.

As we walked down the street, the pastor looked at me. "No one has ever spoken like that to Ben. I have tried but he walks away. He is very stubborn. He heard you though. I will keep trying to get him to come to church."

* * *

After lunch, I suggested we walk over to the football pitch. Since it was Sunday afternoon, many boys would likely be playing—perhaps some fisher boys. Daa joined the pastor at one end of the village and Bridget walked with me.

The village had changed little since my leaving there ten years earlier. I noticed the same buildings, shanties, and huts. Many of the people had surely changed, but they seemed the same men, women, and children that survived on the fishing trade.

I had no nostalgic feeling as one returning to a place they once lived. This village represented enslavement. The end of any innocence I had. I did not hate being there again. I did not love it either. It merely existed.

The football pitch had the same old rusted car at one end serving as a goal. It looked terrible. So many holes and rocks, but when I played there, I likely did not notice. Nine boys ran back and forth kicking a round brown item that likely had been a football in the distant past.

"Hey, you boys, mind if I play?" I asked, walking onto the pitch.

One of the boys, pointing to his chest, said, "I'm Kojo, the captain. You can be on our team."

I supported my team with several strategic passes but could not resist the urge to power a shot into the side of the old rusted car.

"Good shot, Kwaku," Bridget said, with solo applause.

One of the boys picked up the ball and walked up to me. "Hey. I know you. You're Stephen Ghansah. The World Cup hero." He waved for the other players to join us. "It's Kwaku Ghansah."

"Kwaku! Kwaku! Kwaku!" they shouted.

I smiled and moved my hands up and down to quiet them. "Well, I am Stephen Ghansah. People call me Kwaku. And I did play in the World Cup, but I am no hero. I am fortunate to have played with a great team."

"What was it like?" Kojo asked.

"How did you score the winning goal?" asked another.

I held up a finger. "How about I show you?"

I spent the next several minutes demonstrating to the boys some techniques. I had gone to the village to share the Gospel. Spending time with these boys won me an audience with them for kingdom business. Or at least I had hoped it would.

"Eh! Let's go, boys," came a shout from an older boy on the path that led to the lake.

Four of the boys, including Kojo, began walking away.

"You have to quit playing so early?" I asked. "It is still afternoon."

The boys stopped and looked back.

"Our master will only let us play a short time. He wants us to save our energy for fishing," Kojo said.

Another generation of fisherboys, I thought.

"Eh! Let's go! Now!" the voice from the path shouted.

One of the boys pulled at Kojo's arm. "Come, Kojo. Master Lionel will beat us if we are late."

I darted a look back towards the boys. "Did you say, Lionel?"

Kojo nodded. "Yes."

Could this be the same Lionel that bullied me? My fellow fishing slave? I thought there could certainly be more Lionels out there, but I had to investigate.

"I am coming with you. Your master may be an old acquaintance of mine."

I tossed the ball back at the remaining boys. "You practise what I showed you. I will be back soon."

Bridget had been talking with some children near the pitch, likely about Jesus. "Where are you going, Kwaku?"

"I will be back," I said with a wave.

Kojo and the boys with him moved swiftly down the path far ahead of me. I followed them, remembering the path I had walked many times to and from the pitch. The same trail Daa and I took when he told me he intended to adopt me.

I turned the corner and through a clearing saw Master Ben's shanty. Boats lined the shore and a slight breeze cooled me. Several boys sat eating under the large mango tree. A young girl walked back from the tree and into the shanty, likely having served the boys banku.

I stepped in front of the shanty and waved at Kojo. He and the other boys ran over to me. Several shook my hand and we snapped fingers.

A tall man, picking his teeth, walked out of the shanty. "What are you boys doing?" He wore sandals, shorts, and a shirt, unbuttoned all the way down. His right eye, all white, no pupil.

"Lionel? It is you."

"Yeah. I'm Lionel. Who are you?"

"You do not remember me? It is me, Kwaku."

I stood there, void of body language. I did not offer my hand, unsure how I felt about him.

"Ah, Kwaku. The fisherboy turned football star. I remember you." He laughed in mocking tone. "You boys, see this big football star. I remember him. I taught him how to fish. He could not even swim. I had to save him from drowning once."

The boys looked on, no doubt astounded at this odd connection between their master and me.

"Is that how you remember things, Lionel?" I folded my arms. "I believe it was John that taught me how to fish. And, I believe it was Prince that saved me from drowning that day. You remember Prince, do you not?"

Lionel lost his smile. "Who? Prince? I don't remember. So many boys." He began to walk away.

His lies angered me but I kept my composure. Remember why you are here. Remember kingdom work, I said to myself.

A crowd of people gathered around us.

"It is Kwaku Ghansah?" one person whispered.

"It is him," said another.

Apparently, word spread that I had come to the village.

"Lionel, look at this." I pointed to an old upturned boat by the shanty.

Lionel turned back and looked.

"You remember how Ben bent me over this boat and caned me. Prince tackled Ben to defend me and Ben hit him in the head with a paddle, killing him. Ben made you take Prince onto the lake and dump him in the water. I know you remember. I know it affected you."

Lionel shook his head. "I don't remember any of that."

"Fine. You say you do not remember. But God surely does."

The crowd grew. What should have been a private talk between two former slaves had become a spectacle.

"Tell me, Lionel. What happened to John, William, and Ivy? Do you remember them?"

"I don't know. They ran off. Master Ben kept drinking so much, he could not control anyone. He became a bad master. Ivy said she was going back to the North and just walked off one day."

"And John and William?" I asked.

"They took the boat one day and never came back. I guess they drowned. Who cares about them? Now I'm the master."

Lionel picked up an old oar and lifted it up as some sort of instrument of authority. "Everyone leave! Get out of here! You boys, go and fish. Go!"

The boys cowered and ran towards the boats. The crowd backed away but stayed curiously close enough to hear.

"Clean this up!" Lionel yelled at the girl who worked at his shanty.

She began picking up bowls when Lionel kicked her backside. She fell, dropping the bowls everywhere.

"Look what you did, you stupid girl. Pick up this mess."

Lionel turned and walked back to me. "You see, Kwaku. You see what kind of master I am. I'm a good master. They obey me."

Lionel threw the oar down and walked into the shanty. He roared out holding a cane, rage in his eyes.

I backed up a step, thinking I might need to defend myself.

"You see this cane, Kwaku?" he said, waving the cane at me. "This is why they obey me. This is what a good master does."

I placed my hands behind my back. "You do not impress me, Lionel. You are not a good master. You are only one thing. A sinner in desperate need of a merciful God."

His eyes widened and he stepped towards the lake. "Kojo, come here."

The boys had yet to paddle out. Kojo dropped the net he was preparing and ran to Lionel.

Lionel walked back to me. "I will show you what kind of master I am."

Kojo held his head high on the football field but now his head and shoulders drooped in submission.

Lionel grabbed him and threw him down over the old boat. "I will show you what a good master does, Kwaku." Lionel raised the cane to strike Kojo.

"Stop it!" I yelled. "You do not need to do this."

He waved the cane at me. "Yes, I do. You think you are a big man. Big football star. You embarrassed me and called me a liar. They must learn I am in charge."

"Then strike me. I will take Kojo's beating. I will lay over the old boat and you can beat me."

Lionel darted his eyes at me. His teeth clenched; he lowered the cane.

"Beat me, Lionel."

"Ah! That is stupid." Lionel said, looking around at many witnesses. "Kojo, get up. Go fish."

Kojo sprang up and ran to the boat, paddling away.

"Lionel, listen to me. You need to let these boys and girls go. You have no right to force them to do this work."

His mouth dropped open. "Are you crazy, boy? Are you crazy? I paid for them. They owe me many years of work. These boys live with me. Their families don't want them. This is what they do, and I own them. This is how things are done."

"No, Lionel. You do not own anyone. They are slaves. You must let them go."

He threw the cane down. "Who says I must let them go? You? The village chief?

"The God Most High. He has ordained their release. We can take them to the church and ask the pastor to help find their family. Or we can find some suitable place for them to live for now."

"This is crazy talk." Lionel began walking to the shanty. "Leave. Get out of here with that talk."

"OK, Lionel. I will leave. For now. But I will be back. I do not know when or how, but I will be back and these children will be free."

"Ahh," Lionel swiped his hand at me as he walked into the shanty and shut the door.

* * *

I spent the next several months thinking and praying about how I might help those enslaved boys and girls. I certainly trusted God's will and knew he might be calling me to get involved. But what could I do against a system that had been in place for so long? I thought of Kwame Nkrumah and his drive for education, independence, and freedom. I desired that kind of courage.

I travelled with Daa to the Cape Coast one day for his business.

"Kwaku, you should tour Elmina Castle while I conduct my business," Daa said.

I had seen the castle before, but never took the tour. I stood in the cells, horrified at what my African ancestors suffered before their eventual voyage to slavery. Cramped, dark, and dank conditions with little food or water. Treated like animals.

We walked down a corridor to the infamous Door of No Return, the final door slaves walked through as enslavers led them to the ships. Instantly, an eerie feeling overwhelmed me. I welled up with emotion and tears flowed from my eyes. I appreciated my fortune to have been rescued from slavery, given a new life, and that I never journeyed through a door of no return. At that moment, a thought entered my mind.

I could become a Member of Parliament (MP). I could use the seat of government to effect change. Although younger than most MPs, my education and notoriety gave me an advantage.

I had a new dream. Not merely an MP. That was not the dream. But to free slaves and see them adopted. My new dream.

SEVENTEEN

Everyone in the room had wiped away a few tears during Kwaku's story. Especially Ama Danku. More than once during his story, her pencil sat idle as she listened to his tales of being orphaned, enslaved, and finally adopted.

Kwaku placed his hand on top of his wife Grace's hand and lightly stroked it.

"Well, Ms Danku. What do you think of my story?"

Ama leaned forward. "Amazing. Truly amazing. But you know, I have many more questions."

Kwaku chuckled. "Of course you do. Ask away."

Grace stood up. "I'll get us some fresh tea."

"Honourable Ghansah, how did you convince the people to vote for you?" Ama said, as she looked down at her pad, ready to write.

"My current slogan, EVERY GHANAIAN MATTERS. Although I did not use that phrase then, everything I spoke about embodied it. My opponent was and is a good man, but he expressed no passion for the average Ghanaian. He spoke continually about his experience and education. Notable attributes, but things that did not concern the average voter. Reporters asked about my views. They

169

already knew my name from the World Cup and did not seem interested in my upbringing.

"Did you talk about fishing slavery?"

"Not at first. I spoke to the people about their sons and daughters. About what kind of situation your son and daughter could be in if they were orphaned. Where would they live? How would they eat? But slowly, I did talk about our government's role in ending the trafficking of children. Forced fishing and forced prostitution." Kwaku leaned forward, gesturing with his hands. "I even discovered that unscrupulous men, pretending to be sports agents, entice families to give their life savings to send their boys to play football in Europe. Once the boy is there, the agent sells the boy into slavery. I spoke about these things matter-of-factly and considered the life circumstances of my audience. I want a better Ghana for vulnerable children. The cause of freedom and of right."

Grace returned with the tea. "What are you two discussing now?"

"Politics, of course," Ama responded. She turned back to Kwaku. "What about economics and jobs? Everyone wants to know a candidate's position on those issues."

"Oh, we debated those things at length. I have never been a one-issue candidate. But when the opportunity arose, I discussed the plight of orphans and those trafficked. Awareness of these issues are one problem, the system mentality is another. Like the confrontation I told you about with Lionel and me. We have to show that there is a better way. As president, I will have the biggest voice in Ghana. I will fight this system mentality. I will encourage more rescues. Introduce new fishing methods that do not require the work of children. We already have a law in place to outlaw trafficking, but we must enforce it."

"Why is it not enforced?"

"Many reasons. Most of the victims are children and are afraid to testify. I led an investigation into Lionel's operation. We found many of the boys suffering from malnutrition, unhealed broken bones, diseases from the lake water, and cane marks on their backsides. Lionel had impregnated a 14-year-old girl, but she lost the baby after he repeatedly kicked her in the stomach."

Ama shook her head. "We should do something now. Why can't we go rescue them all, right now? Why don't we arrest—"

Kwaku held up his hand. "I wish we could. But we have found a negotiated release to be a better method. Not all these masters are evil. Some of them do not understand it is against the law. We have some wonderful groups that talk to the village chiefs and the masters and convince them that a better life is in store for the children. This allows them to find out a child's story, why they ended up fishing, and potentially leads towards their restoration to a biological family."

"What about the children with no biological family?"

"That is one of the biggest problems. It is very expensive to rehabilitate these children by offering them shelter, education, and parenting. There are group homes but their best option, if biological family is not willing, is adoption."

"Like what the Boatengs did for you?"

Slam!

All three turned towards the front door, which closed so loudly it rattled the walls. Two teen boys walked into the room, one holding a football.

"You do not know what you are talking about. He is the best striker playing today," one said to the other.

"Boys! Quiet please. We have a visitor," Grace said. "Boys, this is Ms Danku. She is interviewing your father."

"You are welcome," they replied, almost simultaneously and walked out of the room. They seemed to have no interest in any of their father's political business.

"I apologise for the interruption. Where were we?"

Ama slowly looked back from where the boys had walked down a hallway to Kwaku. "The Boatengs. They adopted you."

"Yes, but my story is very rare. Most Ghanaians see adopted children with a stigma. This is a mindset we must change. Ghanaians must view adopted children as having as much value as biological children. You saw those two boys. Which one was adopted?"

Ama looked back over at the place they stood earlier. "Uh…I don't know. I know you have five children, three girls and two boys."

"Correct. One of the boys that came in was adopted and one is biological, but we see them the same way. They are both loved and both told to be quiet when necessary."

Ama grinned. "I think I might like to adopt a child some day."

Kwaku grinned back. "And I hope you do. My parents have often spoken in church meetings and to guests in their home on the subject. A few families have adopted, but only a few. I speak frequently about my dreams for Ghana. One of my greatest dreams is that Ghanaians would embrace adoption. Not just for trafficked children, but all orphaned children. Certainly, we want to work hard to find their biological families, but when that is not possible, we should find them loving homes where they have a father and mother to lead them, teach them, and love them."

"And the adoption process is not that difficult," Grace said, leaning forward and talking with her hands. "There are many in social welfare that will help. We tell people all of the time. Call us, we will help you adopt."

"I can see that both of you are passionate about this," Ama said.

Kwaku leaned forward. "We are. And we are as passionate about the family, worried about how they will feed their child. We are concerned with Ghanaians having access to good medical care. We want all villages to have healthy drinking water. Every Ghanaian matters."

Ama nodded, and no one said anything for several seconds. "I understand. I understand much about you now. I have taken a great deal of your time, but I have a few more questions."

"Ask them," Kwaku said, leaning back in his chair.

"Did you ever find out what happened to John and William, the boys you fished with?"

"Yes, actually. About three years after I left, they made the same escape that Prince and I attempted. They waited for a night when Master Ben drank too much and would be too hungover to chase them. They boarded a *trotro* and made it to Accra. John, nearly an adult, found work and insisted that William go to school. A church in Agbogbloshie adopted them. Several of the church families fostered them, gave them shelter and food. Do you remember the William that gave you directions yesterday?"

Ama sprang up. "Was that little William?"

"The one and the same. John is married and works as the assistant manager for a hotel. He is a deacon in our church and has a house full of children. He remains a person of high moral character, and I look up to him."

"And Ivy?"

"I am afraid I never found out what happened to her. She may have gone to the North as Lionel said. I made some inquiries, but I never knew her last name. Like Prince, she is a child lost to slavery. I placed handbills about Prince around Agbogbloshie a few years after my adoption, but no one ever responded. I suppose it was fruitless. No picture. No last name. I had hoped to find his family and let them know what happened to him." Kwaku sighed.

"Did you have another confrontation with Lionel?"

"Let me just say he is out of the fishing business. I heard he lives in another village and works but has no slaves. And old Master Ben died many years ago—defiant and unrepentant."

"Do you still have a relationship with your sister Mercy?"

"Oh yes, of course. We see her often. She married a good man and has three children. She—"

"Kwaku," Grace said.

Kwaku turned and looked at Grace who cocked her head and raised her eyebrows.

Kwaku nodded. "Oh . . . yes. Uh . . . Ms Danku, I would rather this next little bit be off the record.

Ama put her pencil down. "Yes, of course."

"Mercy was angry at God for a long time. I told her many times that she saved my life. Her strength carried us through those terrible days after Mum died. The strength that comes from God. She would argue and say, 'Kwaku, don't you tell me to always look for God.' I always smiled and said, 'but we must.' She carries many scars from what happened. The kind of scars on the inside. But God is healing them one by one. Bridget and my ma . . . our ma, have spent hours and hours talking with her. They have laughed with her and cried with her or simply held her when nothing could be said."

Ama began putting away her things. "Well, Honourable Ghansah, I guess I have no more questions. I suppose I should ask something like why you think you will make a good president, but I think I know the answer. You have much to offer. They really do matter to you, don't they?"

"Every single Ghanaian. With fathers and the fatherless. Slave or free. Old or young. Every one of them."

"Amazing," Ama said. "You will make a great president."

"Ha!" Grace said. "You better be careful or you will give him a big head."

All three laughed and stood up.

"I assure you, Ms Danku, I have many faults."

Grace began clearing the teacups from the table.

"Ms Danku," Kwaku said, "I noticed you have been staring at that old, flattened football on the shelf. You probably are wondering why I have that nasty thing up there."

Grace smiled, "I have wondered that myself, many times."

"Well, yes, I am curious," Ama said.

"Do you remember the football I was given for my 13th birthday?"

"Uh . . . oh, yes. Of course. The one with red pentagons."

"Well, they are no longer red after years of play. That ball has been through so much. It has been beaten, battered, and had changed over the years, but it is my most cherished possession. Like God's grace, I did not earn it. It was given to me. Even in an old football, I always look for God."

www.ingramcontent.com/pod-product-compliance
Lightning Source LLC
Chambersburg PA
CBHW032144170626
46808CB00006B/2359